mary-kateandashley

Sweet 16

Look for these
Sweet 16
titles:

mary-kateandashley

Sweet 16
LOVE AND KISSES

Louise A. Gikow

HarperCollins*Entertainment*
An Imprint of HarperCollins*Publishers*

A PARACHUTE PRESS BOOK

A PARACHUTE PRESS BOOK
Parachute Publishing, LLC
156 Fifth Avenue
Suite 325
NEW YORK
NY 10010

First published in the USA by HarperEntertainment 2002
First published in Great Britain by HarperCollins*Entertainment* 2006
HarperCollins*Entertainment* is an imprint of HarperCollins*Publishers* Ltd,
77-85 Fulham Palace Road, Hammersmith, London W6 8JB

SWEET 16 books are created and produced by Parachute Press, LLC, in
cooperation with Dualstar Publications, a division of Dualstar Entertainment Group,
LLC, published by HarperEntertainment, an imprint of HarperCollins Publishers.

The HarperCollins *Children's Books* website address is
www.harpercollinschildrensbooks.co.uk

1 3 5 7 9 8 6 4 2

The author asserts the moral right to be
identified as the author of the work.

ISBN-13   978 0 00 718107 0
ISBN-10   0 00 718107 8

Printed and bound in Great Britain by Clays Ltd, St Ives plc

chapter one

"Hi! I'm Mary-Kate Olsen, and I have an appointment."

I was standing in the offices of *Girlz* magazine, talking to the girl at the reception desk. She had bright red hair, friendly green eyes, and tons of freckles.

"Who are you here to see?" she asked, looking up at me.

"I'm supposed to meet with Ms. Fein," I told her. "She's the editor in chief—" I stopped, blushing. Why was I telling her who Ms. Fein was? Anyone who worked here would know that!

"Mary-Kate Olsen," the girl repeated. She glanced down at the appointment book that sat open on her desk.

I peered at it and saw my name. "That's me," I said, pointing. "Right there."

"Got it." The girl put a check mark in the book. "I'm Lacey McDonnough," she said, smiling. "Ms. Fein is running a little late, but I'm sure she'll be finished soon. Why don't you take a seat?"

"Thanks." I sat down in one of the plush lime-green chairs and took a deep breath.

Lacey picked up the phone and pressed a button. "Beverly?" she said into the receiver. "C.K.'s five o'clock appointment is here."

I swallowed hard. I couldn't believe I was actually here to interview for a part-time job working for C.K. Fein—editor in chief of the hottest magazine for teens in the whole country!

I looked around. The *Girlz* magazine offices were on the twenty-second floor of a shiny new building in downtown Santa Monica. The reception area was large and airy, with windows on three sides. Against the fourth wall—the one without windows—was the glossy pink reception desk.

The walls were painted a bright purple with wide horizontal stripes that went all the way around the room. Framed covers of the magazine—from the very first issue to last month's—hung on the walls. Looking at them gave me a little thrill. Was it possible that I might actually work on the next issue?

A woman hurried up, dropped an envelope on Lacey's desk, and said, "Would you please call a messenger for this?" She was blond, perfectly made up, and dressed in what had to be a designer suit. She gave me a quick, questioning look before heading back into the inner offices.

I glanced down at my outfit. I was wearing a black blazer, a pink silk shirt I'd borrowed from my sister Ashley, and a flowered skirt. When I got dressed this afternoon for my interview, I thought I looked pretty professional. Now I wasn't so sure.

Lacey made her call to the messenger service, then gave me an encouraging smile. "Hang in there," she said. "I'm sure C.K. will be out in a moment."

"No problem," I told her. "I can use the time to calm myself down."

"You don't look nervous at all."

"That's a relief," I said. "Because my heart is pounding, my mouth is dry, and my stomach feels like it's full of stampeding elephants."

"You really want the job, huh?" Lacey said sympathetically.

"You could say that." I nodded at the nearest row of magazine covers. "I've been reading *Girlz* since I was eleven. Every issue, from cover to cover. I'd give my entire CD collection to work here."

"I totally understand," Lacey said. "I just got my job about four weeks ago, and I still can't believe my luck. Breaking into the magazine business is tough. I must have made a hundred calls before I landed even a single interview."

"Wow," I said. "I guess I was lucky. My high school teacher recommended me for this job. Ms. Barbour. She's a friend of Ms. Fein's. . . ."

"The famous Ms. Barbour." Lacey smiled again. "C.K. talks about her a lot. There's a picture of the two of them on C.K.'s wall, from when they interned together at *Sensation*."

Sensation! I tugged nervously at a strand of my wavy blond hair. *Sensation* was *the* cutting-edge fashion magazine.

"You must have seen a lot of high school kids come in and out of here in the last few days, huh?" I asked Lacey. Maybe she could give me some info about my competition.

"Yeah. There are a lot of applicants for the jobs."

"Jobs?" I said, surprised.

"Uh-huh," Lacey replied. "There are actually two openings."

"Great," I said. "That doubles my chances of getting one of them."

Lacey nodded. Then her green eyes narrowed slightly.

"Is something wrong?" I asked her.

She hesitated for a second. "Not really wrong," she said, "but do you mind my telling you something a little . . . well, personal?"

"No. What is it?"

Lacey got up and walked around the desk. She peered at my pink blouse. "You've got some sort of stain on your blouse. Right there by the collar."

"Huh?" I looked down, but I couldn't see anything.

Lacey opened a drawer in her desk and brought out a makeup mirror. She held it out to me, and I studied my reflection. Sure enough, there, right below the collar of Ashley's beautiful pink silk blouse, was a white stain. What was it? I peered closer and groaned.

Toothpaste!

Just then I heard a loud voice right outside the reception area. "I don't care what the printer thinks," the voice said. "The registration is off. Get them to run it again. And check the other color proofs while you're at it. Now go!"

"Yes, C.K.," a male voice said.

I panicked. C.K. Fein was headed my way, and I had a major white splotch on my blouse!

"Here!" Lacey said. She stood up, whipped a scarf off her neck, and draped it around mine. "It even matches. C.K. will never notice."

I looked at Lacey gratefully. "I owe you," I told her.

"No problem," she said, tying the scarf. She stepped back, admiring her handiwork. "Let me give you some advice," she added quickly. "Let C.K.

do all the talking. Don't mention the dart board. And tell her how much you like Dobermans."

Dart board? Dobermans? What I was getting into?

C.K. Fein strode into the room.

"Your five o'clock appointment, C.K.," Lacey said, "for one of the part-time jobs."

"Mary-Kate Olsen." Ms. Fein looked me up and down as she shook my hand with a strong grip. "C.K. Fein. Hold my calls, okay, Lacey?" she said. "Beverly's busy."

"Yes, C.K.," Lacey answered. She gave me a tiny wink.

C.K. Fein was about Ms. Barbour's age, but she didn't look anything like her. Ms. Barbour always looked crisp and put together. C.K. Fein, on the other hand, was wearing a rumpled gray suit and a pair of scuffed sneakers. Her curly brown hair was pulled back into a ponytail held by a maroon scrunchie with a pencil stuck through it. She wore square, heavy, purple-framed eyeglasses and no makeup.

We walked down a corridor lined with photographs of celebrities and gorgeous models. It reminded me a little of my dad's office. Dad is an executive at Zone Records, and he has signed pictures of his artists hanging all over the place.

Ms. Fein gestured to a door. "Come in," she said. "Sorry for the mess."

Mess was an understatement. The office looked even worse than my room does when I'm pulling an all-nighter. Stacks of magazines and files were scattered all over the floor. An end table held empty coffee mugs and a large table against a wall was covered with photographs. C.K.'s desk was so cluttered with papers that I could hardly see her computer.

But I *could* see the silver-framed photos of two ferocious-looking dogs. *Those are definitely the Dobermans,* I thought. I glanced up. *And there's the dart board.* Six darts were stuck into the board, piercing what looked like some kind of memo. I peered at it, but it was too far away for me to read.

"Sit," Ms. Fein said, pointing to a chair. It had a pile of clothes and magazines on it. I moved them to the end table, then obediently sat, thinking, *This must be how the Dobermans feel.*

Ms. Fein looked at me over the top of her glasses. "So, tell me about yourself. How did you find out about this job? What grade are you in?"

"I'm a sophomore at Bayside High," I said. "Ms. Barbour told me about this job. She's my English teacher. She also manages the school Website, which I—"

"Oh, yes, yes, yes," Ms. Fein cut in. "I have some of your writing samples right here." She pulled a purple file folder from a stack on her desk and opened it. "I liked this one about high school cliques," she went on. "And the one about surviving freshman year was very good. You have talent."

Wow! A real magazine editor was telling me I had talent! I wanted to jump up and cheer, but I knew that wouldn't be cool. I couldn't wait to tell Ashley, though.

"Thank you," I said. "I also have some of my photographs," I added, reaching into my bag. "Before I started writing for the Website, I took photos, and—"

"That's all right," Ms. Fein said. "This job mostly involves filing, proofreading, research, and organizational skills. No taking photos, I'm afraid."

"No problem," I said quickly. "And speaking of photos," I added, remembering what Lacey had said, "those are two beautiful dogs. They're . . . uh . . . Dobermans, right?"

Ms. Fein squinted at me. For a moment I was afraid I had gone over the top. But then her face softened. "This is Fluffy, and this is Peachblossom," she said, pointing to each dog in turn. "My babies."

I couldn't imagine two dogs that looked less like a Fluffy and a Peachblossom. But I just nodded and smiled. "They're very handsome, Ms. Fein."

"Yes, they are," she agreed, smiling lovingly at the photographs. Then she picked up her desk calendar and riffled through it.

"We're putting together our January issue now," she said briskly. "Quick! Give me three ideas for feature stories"—she looked at her watch—"starting now!"

"Ummm . . ."

My mind went blank. Totally blank. I couldn't think of a single thing!

Oh, no, I thought. *Was I about to lose my dream job before it even started?*

chapter two

Think, Mary-Kate! I told myself. I took a deep breath and my brain came back on-line.

"Okay," I said, looking at the photos of Fluffy and Peachblossom, "how about . . . an article about what you can tell about people from their pets? Instead of knowing what sign they are or what movies they like . . . sort of a personality test. It could have a page showing celebrities—actors, athletes, maybe even famous writers—with their pets."

Ms. Fein's eyebrows arched up over the purple rims of her glasses. I couldn't tell if that was a good reaction or a bad one.

"And here's another idea," I went on before I lost my courage. "We could interview girls whose best friends are boys. The article could be about how it's totally different from having a boyfriend or close girlfriends. What you can and can't talk to them about. And for a third story—"

"Time's up," Ms. Fein said.

"But I only gave you two ideas."

"They were enough," Ms. Fein replied. She stood up and held out her hand.

I felt my throat getting tight. *There goes my dream job*, I thought, shaking her hand.

"Call me C.K. Your hours are from three to five on Tuesdays, Wednesdays, and Thursdays," she said, "though you'll probably have to stay late some days."

I stared at her.

"Is there a problem?" she asked.

"I-I just want to make sure I understand. You mean, you're hiring me?"

"You just proved to me that you can think fast on your feet. Those were both good ideas for feature articles."

I was so shocked, I couldn't say anything for a moment. Luckily that didn't seem to bother C.K.

"The job starts tomorrow," she said. "I expect you to be on time. It's not glamorous—no big parties, no celebrities, no discounts on clothing. It's hard work. But you'll learn about the magazine business from the ground up. If you're very lucky and very good, I might let you do a little writing."

She was really offering me the job! "It sounds great to me," I said.

"So. Three tomorrow. Can you make it?"

"Sure, Ms. Fein—I mean, C.K.! You bet!" I said.

"Good. Lacey can show you around when you get here. Congratulations! And welcome to *Girlz* magazine, Mary-Kate."

C.K.'s phone rang. She snatched it up and waved me out the door. I floated out to the reception area in a daze.

Lacey looked up. "How'd it go?" she asked.

"I got the job!" I said. "I start tomorrow."

"Congratulations!" Lacey said. "So, I guess I'll see you tomorrow!"

"Definitely," I said. "Oh, before I forget—" I took off her scarf and gave it back to her. "Thanks again. I really appreciate it!"

I stood in the elevator, my head whirling. I had just landed a job at *Girlz* magazine! *Woo-hoo!*

❀

I pushed open the door to Click Café and glanced at my watch. Uh-oh. It was 5:25. I was late for my date with Aaron.

Click was filled with kids from school. "Hey, Ashley!" My friend, Lauren Glazer, waved to me. I waved back.

Lauren and her boyfriend, Ben Jones, were holding hands across a rickety wooden table. Some other friends—Brittany Bowen, Melanie Han, and Tashema Mitchell—were gathered around one of the computers. I finally spotted my boyfriend, Aaron, on the old blue-flowered sofa near the window.

I hurried over to him. He looked up at me, and his wavy, dark hair flopped over his forehead. He pushed it back impatiently with his right hand.

"I know, I know!" I said before he could say anything. "I was the one who made the date. I was the one who made a fuss about meeting at exactly five on the dot. And I'm the one"—I looked at my watch—"who is exactly twenty-six minutes late."

"Twenty-seven by that clock over there," Aaron pointed out.

"It's fast," I said, leaning over to give him a kiss.

"Sure it is." Aaron smiled.

I flopped onto the sofa next to him. "I *am* sorry," I said in a rush. "It was the first meeting for the Valentine's Day dance. Nobody wanted to focus. All they could talk about were the auditions for the school play and how well the basketball team is doing. So I finally had to take over. Once we really got started, though, we had a ton of ideas. And wait till you hear the big one!"

I caught Malcolm Freeman's eye and waved. Malcolm works at Click in the afternoons. He wandered over.

"Hey, Malcolm," I said. "Could I get a decaf mocha latte, please?"

"Make sure it's decaf," Aaron said. "I don't think Ashley needs any more caffeine right now."

I gave him a look. But I couldn't stay mad at Aaron for more than three seconds.

Malcolm saluted and wandered back to the counter. He was obviously in one of his uncommunicative moods.

"Anyway," I went on, "Valentine's Day is on a Friday this year, so we're going to hold the dance the next night. And I had this incredible idea! You know those adorable old-fashioned pictures of little cupids and angels? They're all pink and precious, with tiny bows and arrows and hearts and things?"

"I think so. . . ." Aaron said.

"Well, we're decorating the whole gym with cupids and little angels just like that. I've got some pictures of Victorian Valentine's Day cards, and we're going to blow them up and hang them. There'll be puffy cotton clouds all over the ceiling and a big pink ribbon bow right over the stage. And guess why?"

"Why?" Aaron asked.

"Because the entertainment for the dance is going to be—Angelica Velasquez! That's my plan, anyway."

"Angelica Velasquez?" Aaron sat up straight. "Angel? Ashley, she's really hot! But how are you going to get Angel to sing at a high school dance?"

"My secret weapon, of course," I said. "My dad." My father knows every singing star in the world because of his job. I just knew he'd be able to help me get Angel for our dance.

"So," I continued, "the whole dance will be themed around Angel. Isn't that a great idea?"

"If you can pull it off, it'll be something." Aaron put an arm around my shoulders and hugged me. "And if anyone can pull it off, Ashley, you can."

I hugged him back. "What do you say to a double date with Lauren and Ben before the dance? We could all go together. We could even rent a limo! Then Sophie and Malcolm could come along, too. And Mary-Kate and Brittany and their dates. Maybe we could have dinner at that neat new Vietnamese-French restaurant and—"

"Whoa!" Aaron held a hand up. "Slow down. First of all, the Valentine's Day dance is—what? Almost two months away? Besides, did it ever occur to you that I might have some ideas of my own about how we should spend Valentine's Day?"

"I'm sorry!" I said. "You're right. I guess I was caught up in planning mode because of the meeting. What do *you* want to do?"

Aaron thought for a minute. "How about Capretto's? It would be kind of romantic. You know, spending Valentine's Day at the place we had our first date."

The idea made me smile. "Oh, Aaron, that's so incredibly sweet. But Capretto's is all the way on the other side of town. And we wouldn't have enough time to really enjoy ourselves if we had to rush off to the dance right after dinner. I'm going to have to be at school early that night to make sure things are on track."

"Then how about Le Shack? That's only ten minutes away. And they have awesome seafood."

"Le Shack is great," I agreed, "but it's sort of messy to eat there. It's the kind of place you go wearing shorts and a T-shirt. And you wear bibs so you don't get clam juice and stuff all over you. And we'll be all dressed up—"

Aaron shook his head. "I give up. Why don't you just go ahead and plan everything? I'll come along for the ride."

Malcolm brought me my latté, but I barely noticed. I was staring at Aaron. *Come along for the ride?* What did he mean by that? "Is something wrong?" I asked.

Aaron's face cleared. "No. It's okay. I just thought . . . oh, never mind."

"Are you sure?" Now that I thought about it, Aaron had seemed a little touchy lately.

"Positive." He gave me a quick kiss and stood up. "I'm going to get one of those brownies in the case. Wanna split it?"

"Um . . . sure. Just a bite, though."

Aaron got in line at the counter, and I went back to planning the dance. There was so much to focus on: Angel, the decorations, the food. This Valentine's Day just had to be the best one ever. And I was going to make sure it was!

❀

"Get me a coffee, Mary-Kate, would you? Black," C.K. snapped as she raced past my desk. Today she had traded in her wrinkled gray suit for a wrinkled brown one. The scrunchie and the pencil were still in place.

It was Wednesday afternoon, my first day on the job, and the staff of *Girlz* was in high gear. People rushed around from office to office, calling out to one another in the halls. The phones were ringing nonstop. I had already seen one semi-celebrity—a girl from one of the soaps. C.K.'s assistant, Beverly, was interviewing her for the February issue.

I was sitting at my very own desk across the hall from C.K.'s office. I had my very own file cabinets, my very own telephone, and my very own computer. But I hadn't used any of them yet. It was almost five o'clock, and so far all I had done was make three pots of coffee and about a thousand photocopies.

I wondered if I was going to be spending all my working hours making coffee and copies. I sighed and shook my head. Well, if that's the way it was, I'd deal with it. I'd make a million cups of coffee and a zillion copies if I had to. But I'd do it with my ears open. I was here to learn, and that's exactly what I was going to do.

"Mary-Kate?" C.K. stuck her head out of Viv's office. Viv is the magazine's beauty editor. "Could you come in here for a minute?"

I poked my head into the office. C.K. and Viv were arguing about some photographs.

"She looks terrible," C.K. was saying. "We're going to have to reshoot. Maybe with a different model this time."

"I know." Viv sighed. "I already told Jack." She turned to me. "Oh, Mary-Kate. Would you run over to the Crashbox Cosmetics offices? I need you to pick up a batch of new blush samples." She winked at me. "They're for C.K. here."

"I don't have time to put on blush," C.K. snapped. "I'm too busy. Unlike everyone else in this office."

"Of course," Viv said, grinning.

She handed me a piece of paper. On it was the address of Crashbox—a cool new cosmetics company. Their offices and the makeup factory were over on Whittier. "Ask for Ms. Fischer," Viv told me as I headed out.

"I'll be back A.S.A.P.," I promised.

Ms. Fischer at Crashbox was really nice. She even gave me a few eye shadows and some mascara to take home with me. When I got back to the office, I dropped the blush samples off with Viv's assistant and then headed to the ladies' room to touch up my own makeup. I had to try that new Crashbox PowerPurple mascara. Then I stopped at the reception desk to say hello to Lacey.

"So, how's your first day going?" she asked me.

"Okay, I hope," I said. I lowered my voice to a whisper. "But I don't know how well I'm going over with C.K. She's, uh, interesting."

"Don't worry," Lacey whispered. "It's not you. C.K. can be a terror. The last assistant she had before Beverly was Kim. Well, Kim discovered she was going to have a baby. But for the entire nine months she was too afraid to tell C.K. about it. Everybody else in the office knew . . . but not C.K.

"The last month Kim was here," Lacey went on, "C.K. called Kim into her office. 'Putting on a little weight, I see,' she said. Poor Kim was petrified! But C.K. had actually arranged a surprise baby shower for her. Kim told me she was so freaked out, it was a wonder she didn't have the baby right there!"

"That was sweet of her," I said.

Lacey nodded. "She's really a decent person. Plus she knows her stuff. She founded the magazine all by herself about ten years ago. She supposedly walked into the office of the head of Harris Publications and sold him on the idea in five minutes flat. Ever since then this place has been her life. She works all day, and she goes on-line and talks to a special panel of kids for hours each night to really get inside their heads. She's completely devoted to *Girlz*."

"How about you?" I asked. "How do you feel about being here?"

"Well, being a receptionist isn't exactly my dream job," Lacey admitted. "I studied layout and design in college. There weren't any jobs in the art department, so I took this one. My boyfriend thinks I'm crazy to sit behind this desk all day, but it pays the rent. Plus I'm hoping this job will be a stepping-stone to something bigger." Lacey crossed her fingers on both hands. "I keep hoping someone will remember what my qualifications are and move me out of here."

I knew how Lacey felt. I'd do almost anything to prove to C.K. Fein that I wasn't just another high school kid. I knew I could write. All I needed was a chance.

As I was heading out the door that afternoon, C.K. intercepted me. "Good job today, Mary-Kate," she said.

"Thanks, C.K." *I guess she liked my coffee.* "If you want, you can call me M.K.," I added. "You know, like C.K.?"

C.K. totally ignored my suggestion. "Our other part-timer is starting tomorrow, Mary-Kate," she said, "so you won't have to make *all* the coffee from now on." She rushed off.

I blinked. Had C.K. Fein read my mind?

I had to admit, it would be nice to have another person around the office to help make the coffee. I wondered what she would be like.

chapter three

The next afternoon I got to the *Girlz* magazine offices a little early. Lacey was busy signing for a package when I came through the doors. As I waited to say hi, I glanced around the room. I couldn't help but notice the cute guy who was sitting in one of the lime-green chairs. He had straight, really short black hair, high cheekbones, and blue eyes. He looked about my age. I tried not to stare.

I wonder who he is. . . .

The messenger left. Lacey looked up and smiled. "Hey, Mary-Kate," she said.

"Hi, Lacey. What's up?" I said.

At that moment C.K. strode into the room. She looked over at the cute guy. "Liam," she said, "come with me."

"Yes, ma'am," he said, getting up and walking toward C.K.

"It's C.K.," C.K. said. "If I ever hear you call me *ma'am* again, you're fired."

"You got it, C.K.," Liam said. He followed C.K. into the hallway.

"Who was *that*?" I asked Lacey, leaning over her desk.

"That's Liam McCaffrey," she told me. "He's from Harrison High. He's the guy who got the other part-time job."

My mouth dropped open. "A guy? Working at *Girlz* magazine?"

"Actually, I think it's a great idea," Lacey said. "It'll be good to have another guy around here. The only other males in the office are Jack and Axel."

Jack, the art director, is around my parents' age. Axel is the music editor. He was hardly ever around.

"Besides," Lacey added, "he's kind of cute. Don't you think?"

Lacey had a point. What could be bad about having a good-looking guy around the office?

Plenty, as it turned out.

On the next Tuesday afternoon, while I was grinding espresso beans, I overheard Liam and Amy, the fashion editor, talking by the copy machine.

"You've got a point," Amy was saying. "So write me some sample captions by the end of the day Friday. Maybe I'll be able to use them."

"Great!" Liam said. "I'll E-mail them to you by Wednesday morning."

Sample captions? Liam had a writing assignment already? I shook my head. Talk about beginner's luck.

"Hey, Mary-Kate," Liam said from behind me. I jumped. "Could I get a cup of coffee?"

"Sure." I handed him the empty pot. "Why don't I teach you how to make it yourself? Then you'll be ready if anyone asks."

"Great," Liam said. "Just show me where the water goes. In here?" He pointed to the wrong place on the machine.

"Nope, here. The coffee filters are in that drawer," I explained. "You put one in the machine like this."

"Got it," Liam said, looking at the filter as if he'd never seen one before.

I had to admit, he had great eyes. They were a very light blue rimmed with black, and he had really long lashes, too.

"Sorry I didn't offer to help before," Liam said. "I figured you were making the coffee because you were really good at it."

I looked at him. Was he serious? Anyone could make coffee. I gave him a coffee-making lesson and left him to it.

A while later I poured some coffee into C.K.'s favorite mug—it had pictures of Doberman puppies on it—and headed into her office with some copies she'd asked for.

"Anything else I can do?" I asked.

C.K. gulped down some coffee. Then she made a face. "Who made this?" she asked. "You?"

"No, Liam did," I told her.

C.K. shook her head. "Undrinkable. This office runs on coffee, Mary-Kate. Don't ever let him near that machine again."

C.K. made me queen of the coffee bean from then on. I was stuck—Mary-Kate Olsen, brew editor of *Girlz* magazine.

Somehow I couldn't help wondering if Liam had made that terrible coffee on purpose.

"But you have to let us see him!" I said. "You just have to!"

Lauren and I were standing in the office of Dominick D'Andrea, Angel Velasquez's agent. I'd gotten Mr. D'Andrea's address from my dad's Palm Pilot. Dad has the numbers and addresses of all the agents in Los Angeles in his Palm.

According to the little sign on her desk, the receptionist's name was Ms. Steele. It fit. She was—made of steel, that is. And she wasn't going to bend an inch.

"I'm very sorry, Ashley," she said. "I have a list of all Mr. D'Andrea's appointments, and your name isn't on it. I can't let just anyone in to see him."

"I understand," I said. "But we're here with a business proposition. We want to ask Mr. D'Andrea if Angel would sing at our high school Valentine's Day dance. We'll pay her, of course. I'm sure if he just heard about it—"

"He's not going to hear about it," she said.

"Excuse me," Lauren said. She gave Ms. Steele one of her sweetest smiles. With her clear blue eyes, wavy brown hair, and sprinkling of freckles, Lauren can be hard to resist. "We don't want to be a bother. It will only take a minute to explain—"

"Listen, dear," said Ms. Steele in a slightly gentler tone. "It's my job to make sure that no one goes back there without an appointment. I'm sorry, but that's the way it is."

Lauren tugged at my arm. "We'd better go," she whispered. "Maybe we can book another band—"

I shook my head. "I'm not going anywhere until I speak to Mr. D'Andrea," I said firmly.

I couldn't leave until I'd spoken to Angel's agent. If I didn't, we could totally give up on the idea of having Angel at the dance. And I wasn't ready to do that.

Just then a tanned, slender man walked into the office. He had slicked-back brown hair and was dressed in an ultra-elegant suit. He reached over the top of the reception desk and picked up a stack of messages. "Anything else, Grace?" the man asked Ms. Steele.

"Nothing, Mr. D'Andrea," she said.

I turned and stared. Mr. D'Andrea! What luck! This was my chance, and I was going to take it.

Before he could open the door to his office, I stepped in front of him. "Hi, Mr. D'Andrea," I said politely. "My name is Ashley Olsen, and this is my friend Lauren Glazer."

Mr. D'Andrea paused, his hand on the doorknob. "You look familiar. . . ." He snapped his fingers. "I know, you're Mark Olsen's daughter. And you have a sister, don't you?"

"That's right." I started to feel hopeful. "Her name is Mary-Kate."

Mr. D'Andrea nodded. "I met you girls at a birthday party once when you were about three. One of you threw a handful of birthday cake into my lap. Chocolate, as I recall."

"It wasn't me!" I said quickly, blushing.

"It doesn't matter." Mr. D'Andrea smiled. "I never did like that suit anyway. And I love chocolate cake. So. What are you doing here?"

"Well, actually, we're here to talk to you," I said. My heart was racing with excitement. I could tell we were about two seconds away from getting what we'd come for.

I went on. "You see, I had this totally great idea for my high school's Valentine's Day dance. We want to hire Angel to sing at it. We're going to theme the whole thing around her. We'll have little angels all over the place and—"

"It sounds great, Ashley," Mr. D'Andrea interrupted me. "But Angel can't perform at high school functions. She's just too busy. And if she showed up at yours, I'd get calls begging for her from every school in the country. I'm really sorry, but I'm going to have to say no."

I couldn't believe he was turning us down, just like that!

Lauren spoke up. "Won't you at least ask her, Mr. D'Andrea?"

"Again, I'm sorry, but it's out of the question. Give your father my regards, Ashley." And with that Mr. D'Andrea opened the door to his office and disappeared inside.

"Well, at least he was nice about it," Lauren said. "Sort of."

"He wasn't nice enough," I said. "He's not going to talk to Angel."

"So who are we going to get to sing at the dance?" Lauren asked as we walked outside.

"Angel," I told her.

"But Angel's agent just turned us down. You said yourself that her agent was the only person who could get to her."

28

"Did I?" I said. "Well, I was wrong. There has to be another way, and I'm going to find it. Angel is going to perform at Bayside High's Valentine's Day dance or . . . or . . . I'm not Ashley Olsen!"

chapter four

Another cup of coffee, Dad?"

"Why, yes. Thanks, Ashley." Dad looked up from his newspaper and smiled at me. "This is quite a treat."

I shrugged. "Well, Dad, you work hard. You deserve it."

It was Saturday morning—three days after I'd met Mr. D'Andrea. Dad was lying in bed with a tray on his lap. On the tray was a plate piled high with French toast and maple syrup—his favorite brunch. I had put two bright yellow tulips in a vase and set them on the tray, too. Next to them was a blue glass bowl filled with sliced peaches, mangoes, and papaya.

"So, Ashley," Dad said, finally putting down the newspaper and setting the tray on his night table. "What's the occasion? You haven't made me breakfast in bed since my birthday when you were twelve years old. And, as I recall, you spilled cereal all over the blanket that time." Dad grinned at me. "I think it was Mary-Kate who overturned the pot of coffee."

I blushed. "Okay, I confess. I have a big favor to ask you."

Dad nodded. "I had a feeling there was something."

"Not that I don't think you deserve to be treated this way every morning—" I added quickly.

"I know I do." Dad grinned. "But I also understand that neither of you girls has the time to make me breakfast in bed every day. Plus I don't have the time to eat it. So what can I do for you?"

"Okay." I took a deep breath. "You know how I'm the head of the Valentine's Day dance committee? Well, I had this totally terrific idea. I want to get Angel to sing at the dance."

Dad put one hand up in the air. "Ashley, you know I can't—" he began.

"Dad, wait," I said in a rush. "Let me finish. Angel would be perfect. Her music is so romantic. Plus she's really hot right now. And all the kids are really excited about getting her. I can't let them down.

"Anyway," I continued, "I got in to see Angel's agent, Mr. D'Andrea—he says hi, by the way—but he says it's out of the question. He won't even talk to

Angel about it. So I thought that you might be able to give me her phone number or her E-mail address. I wouldn't ask you to make the call or anything. I'll do it all myself. I just want a chance to ask her. And I can't if I don't know how to reach her."

Dad sighed. "Ashley, you should know better," he said. "All my recording artists—*any* recording artist—deserve to have privacy. If I gave out their phone numbers or addresses to anyone who asked—"

"But I'm not anyone, Dad. I'm me!" I said desperately.

Dad just looked at me.

After a moment I looked down, picking at the white chenille bedspread. "Okay," I said finally. "I know. I'm wrong. I didn't really think you'd tell me. It was a long shot, but I had to try."

Dad smiled. "I understand," he said. "You don't want to let your friends down." He thought for a moment. "You know, I'm pretty sure I read something yesterday about Angel doing a signing of her CDs at a local music store. As I recall, it was happening sometime this week."

I immediately got what he was driving at. "Dad, you're a genius! I'll go down there and have her sign a CD! Then I can ask her to sing at Bayside High!"

"If you're lucky, you might get a moment to state your case," Dad said. "But don't be disappointed if she says no. Though I have to admit, given your powers of persuasion, you might have a chance."

"I'm not *that* persuasive," I told him, giving him a kiss on the forehead. "I couldn't get you to give me Angel's phone number. But I know you're right. And this way is even better! I'm going to go on-line right away and find out which record store Angel's going to be at."

I grabbed Dad's tray and raced down the stairs. I knew that if I could talk to Angel for even a minute, I could convince her to perform at Bayside High. I was sure of it!

❀

The Tuesday after the coffee disaster Liam spent most of the afternoon with C.K.'s assistant, Beverly. It seemed as if every time Liam said something, Beverly laughed. Beverly had a very loud laugh. It was hard to pay attention to the captions I was proofreading for the February fashion spread while Beverly was laughing.

They were Liam's captions, I might add.

On Wednesday C.K. brought her dogs into work. When I got there at three, the first thing I had to do was refill their water bowls.

"Aren't they gorgeous?" C.K. said proudly. The dogs trotted over to me. One of them—I couldn't tell if it was Fluffy or Peachblossom—

jumped up and put her paws on my shoulders. She panted in my face. She was *huge*, and she had serious dog breath. I tried to ignore it and rubbed her ears.

"Down, Peachblossom," C.K. said. "Down!"

So that's who it was. Just then Liam peeked around C.K.'s door. "Hey!" he said happily. "You must be Peachblossom! And you're Fluffy!"

I couldn't believe it. He actually got it right.

The dogs trotted happily over to him to investigate.

"Down," he said. He sounded just like C.K. "Sit. Stay. Good girls!"

"You're a dog person," C.K. said approvingly.

"Yeah. I have two golden retrievers," Liam told her. He was scratching Fluffy behind the ears. Or was it Peachblossom?

C.K.'s eyes lit up. "I had a golden when I was a girl," she said. She glanced at me. "Mary-Kate? Coffee, please."

I left them talking dogs. When I got back with C.K.'s coffee, they were still talking dogs. It seemed as if Liam was in C.K.'s office almost the whole afternoon, playing with Peachblossom and Fluffy. When I went in at around five o'clock to bring C.K. some layouts from Jack, Liam was still there. What's more, now he was tossing darts at C.K.'s dart board. And C.K. was smiling!

She looked up when I knocked. "I'm glad you're here, Mary-Kate," she said. "I wanted to talk to the both of you. Sit."

We both sat. So did Peachblossom and Fluffy.

"I took a look at the lead story for our February issue last night, and it's terrible," C.K. said. "We don't have enough time to assign a new writer. So I'm going to give you two a chance to come up with something."

My heart gave a little jump. A chance to write a real article for the magazine! I stole a glance at Liam. He was leaning back in his chair, his legs stretched out in front of him. He rubbed the top of Peachblossom's head—or was it Fluffy? He looked completely relaxed.

"I want you each to come up with several ideas for a Valentine's Day article," C.K. went on. "I'll choose the best one from each of you, and then you can write it up. Whoever does the best job will get his—or her—story published."

I couldn't believe it. This was my dream come true! I could just see my byline now—

"Mary-Kate? Hello? Mary-Kate?" C.K.'s voice cut through my dreamy haze. "Got any thoughts?"

I woke up from my daydream. "Uh . . . let's see," I stammered. I knew I had to make this good. "How about . . . 'How to Find Your Perfect Valentine'? My sister, Ashley, has an on-line dating service—"

"Sorry, Mary-Kate," C.K. said. "We just did a survey of dating services. It would sound like a rehash."

"Well, uh, what about a story on Valentine's Day makeup? How to really look special for that special someone?"

C.K. shook her head. "That's the kind of thing we cover in the beauty section all the time."

I thought hard. "Then . . . how about 'My Best Valentine's Day Ever?' I could interview people about their happiest Valentine's Day."

"I don't think so," C.K. said. "Those best-ever pieces always end up a little on the sappy side." She turned to Liam. "How about you, Liam? Any ideas?"

Liam stopped scratching Peachblossom's—or was it Fluffy's?—ears. Peachblossom whined.

"How about an article about what your boy-friend would *really* like you to get him for Valentine's Day?" he suggested. "It would be written from a guy's perspective. And it could include a list of stuff guys really want—not the stuff you girls *think* we want."

C.K. pulled the pencil out of her scrunchie and started doodling on a pad of paper. "I like it!" she said. "Why don't you get on it, Liam? I'll need a draft by next Tuesday."

The phone rang. C.K. snatched it up. "Yes? Yes? No, I hadn't read that—what are you talking about?" She picked up a dart from her desk and lobbed it angrily at the dart board.

Thwack! It hit the bull's-eye. Someone was really annoying C.K. The angrier she got, the better her aim was.

She covered the receiver with one hand. "That's it for now. Liam, get on it. Mary-Kate, get back to me with some more ideas by tomorrow. The deadline is tight on this one."

C.K. went back to the phone. Liam and I left her office. The dogs looked after Liam sadly.

"Hey, Mary-Kate," Liam said as he turned down the hall, "if you want to toss some ideas around—"

"Thanks, but I'll figure something out," I said.

"No problem-o," Liam said as he disappeared around a corner. "Just trying to be friendly . . . "

Friendly? I wondered. Liam was being friendly, all right. But I had noticed that he was usually friendly to the people in the office who could help him in some way. People like C.K. and Viv and even Beverly.

Anyway, it didn't matter. I was going to come up with an article all on my own. And it was going to be so brilliant, it would be a lock for the February issue!

Now all I had to do was figure out what it was.

chapter five

"Ashley, I can't believe the line is this long already!" Lauren said.

Lauren and I were standing in front of Friendly Fred's Music Emporium. It was four whole hours before Angel was due to sign CDs and two hours before the store opened. But even this early on a Saturday morning there were already about fifty people waiting, all clutching their Angel CDs, just like we were.

A huge poster of Angel hung in the record-store window. Even though it showed her dressed like any high school kid—in low-rise jeans and a tank top—she looked amazing, with long, curly brown hair, sparkling brown eyes, and a mischievous smile.

Lauren stared at the poster. "Do you think there's any chance we can actually get her?"

"Absolutely," I told her. "Otherwise we wouldn't be here."

The store opened at ten. Angel showed up at 12:45—which was forty-five minutes late. Once the line started moving, though, it moved pretty quickly.

Angel really had this signing thing down. She'd scribble her name, say a quick word, and smile. Then her publicist would gently push one star-struck teen away and move another into place for the next signature.

"These shoes are *killing* me," Lauren muttered under her breath, standing first on one foot and then the other. "Why, oh, why did I have to wear heels? I *knew* we'd be waiting here for hours!"

"Because you just got them, and they're cute, and you look great in them," I told her.

Lauren smiled at me. "You have a point," she said. She looked down at her shoes. "They are pretty cool."

The line moved forward, and we moved along with it.

I wondered if my plan would actually work. That publicist looked pretty determined to keep things short and sweet. I'd have to talk fast.

Lauren took one foot out of a shoe and wriggled her toes. "I can't wait for Valentine's Day," she said dreamily. "Slow dancing to Angel's music—that's the best."

"Oh, that reminds me," I said. "I had this great idea. Why don't we all rent a limo—you and Ben and Malcolm and Sophie and me and Aaron? And Mary-Kate and Brittany and their dates? We could eat at that new Vietnamese-French restaurant."

"Sounds perfect!" Lauren said.

"*I* thought so, too." I frowned. "I just wish Aaron did."

"Doesn't he?" Lauren asked, surprised.

"I don't know," I admitted. "Aaron didn't seem too into the idea. He suggested a few other things. They were really sweet, of course, but none of them made sense. And lately, every time I bring up Valentine's Day, he goes sort of blank on me and says 'Whatever.' Like he doesn't even care *what* we do."

"Of course he cares," Lauren said. "You know Aaron loves you. But guys can never think ahead, and Valentine's Day is a while away. What if he's got something else on his mind? Maybe it's something at home or in school that he's upset about."

"I don't think so," I said, shaking my head. "I wish I knew what was going on."

The line moved forward. I looked up. There were only three kids ahead of us now.

Then two.

Then one.

Then . . .

"Next!" said the publicist.

We stepped forward and dumped our Angel CDs onto the table.

Angel smiled up at us. In person she was even more gorgeous than her poster. "I'm afraid I can't sign all of these," she said apologetically. "Why don't you each choose one?"

Wow. She was also totally nice! I pushed one of my favorites—*Love Letters A to Z*—over to her. Then I cleared my throat.

"Angel?" I said. "We're not here just for the signing. We wanted to invite you to sing at our Valentine's Day dance."

"I'm really sorry," she said at once, "but my agent handles all my concert appearances—"

"I know," I said quickly. "Dominick D'Andrea. We spoke to him. But he wouldn't even ask you. And we thought if we could at least talk to you for a minute—"

Angel's publicist cleared his throat. He looked annoyed. "Time's up, girls," he said. "Next!"

I stood firm. "Angel, the kids at Bayside High are really counting on me to get you to sing," I begged. "Won't you at least consider it?"

Angel's eyes lit up. "Did you say Bayside High?"

"That's our school," Lauren said.

"My parents both went to Bayside High!"

41

Angel exclaimed. "Dad never stops telling us stories about all the stuff he did there. Supposedly his football team has some trophies in the display case in the front hall. From around 1977, I think. And that's where he met my mom—at a Valentine's Day dance." Angel smiled. "She was a sophomore when he was a senior. She hated football. But she thought my dad was cute."

Angel picked up her bag and reached inside. She pulled out a pen, scribbled something on a piece of paper, and handed it to me.

"This is my cell-phone number," she said. "I'd love to sing at your school. It'll give my folks a chance to go back and relive some great memories."

I couldn't believe our luck. "Thank you so much!" I said. "This is so incredibly nice of you!"

"We totally appreciate it!" Lauren chimed in.

Angel's publicist stepped in front of us. "Next!" he said in a loud voice.

Lauren and I moved out of the way, grabbing our CDs as we went.

"You did it, Ashley!" Lauren whooped as we left the store. "Angel is coming to sing at Bayside High!"

"I can't believe it!" I shrieked.

Things were positively perfect. Wait till everybody at school heard! And wait till I told Aaron. He'd be thrilled!

Actually, now that I thought about it, the whole Angel thing might be why he was acting so strangely. I knew I hadn't paid much attention to him in the last few weeks. I'd been too caught up in getting Angel for the dance.

But now that was all set, I was going to focus on Aaron. Before too long everything would be back to normal between us. I was sure of it!

❀

On Thursday I'd given C.K. a whole list of Valentine's Day article ideas. She rejected every single one. Now it was Tuesday. Liam probably had his article finished already. But I wasn't giving up. I had one more idea.

"We could call it 'Love and Kisses: Are You the Perfect Couple?'" I explained to C.K. "I'd interview three perfect couples—kids I know who have great relationships. Maybe we could even have a Perfect Couple contest. The couple that writes the best letter to the magazine wins something. A perfect date, maybe."

C.K. sat back in her chair. "I like it," she said. "Giveaways are always popular. I'll check out the contest with our lawyers. I'm sure we can figure out something.

"You can start talking to people right away," she went on. "Just make sure your perfect couples have some interesting stories to tell. Details, details. Up close and personal. That's what makes a good article."

I almost flew out of C.K.'s office. I was in! And I knew just who I was going to interview: my sister and Aaron, Lauren and Ben, and Malcolm and Sophie. Three perfect couples!

I almost ran smack into Liam. He and Viv were walking down the hall toward me. "I'll write up those descriptions and E-mail them to you tomorrow," he said.

"You're a lifesaver!" Viv said. She ducked into her office as Liam continued down the hall.

I gritted my teeth. I was going to write rings around him. And when the ink was dry, it was going to be Mary-Kate Olsen's article in *Girlz* magazine—not Liam McCaffrey's!

chapter six

Excerpts from the Transcript of Mary-Kate's Interview Tape: "Love and Kisses: Are You the Perfect Couple?"

Interview Number One: Ashley Olsen

MARY-KATE: Is this thing on? Testing. One, two, three, testing. Okay. So, Ashley, do you think you are Aaron are the perfect couple?

ASHLEY: I don't know about perfect, but a girl would have to be crazy not to fall in love with Aaron. He's soooo cute! Not to mention nice and smart and funny. We have lots of things in common, too.

MARY-KATE: Like what?

ASHLEY: Well, he likes sports, and I like to watch him play sports! (LAUGHS.) No, really. We do have lots in common. We both like old movies. We both like listening to music. And poetry. Sometimes he even writes me poetry. It's totally romantic.

MARY-KATE: What else do you like about him?

ASHLEY: I love the way he is with his little sister. I mean, he's so tall and strong, but he's so gentle and sweet with her. The funny thing is, there are times when I actually feel stronger than he is. . . . You know, sometimes I think Aaron gets a little annoyed with me, Mary-Kate. Especially when I want to do something and he maybe wants to think about it some more. I guess I just make up my mind about stuff quicker than he does.

MARY-KATE: So what do you think makes a perfect couple?

ASHLEY: I think it's just something that happens when you're together. You look at each other and you just melt inside. I mean, Aaron and I just fit somehow. We understand each other. We have all these little private jokes and stuff. I really do love him. And I know he loves me. . . .

Interview Number Two: Aaron Moore

MARY-KATE: So, Aaron. What first attracted you to my sister?

AARON: It must be her personality. I mean, it certainly wasn't her looks! Who needs a gorgeous girlfriend with long blond hair and big blue eyes and a great smile? Hey, is that tape recorder really on?

Okay, seriously. I liked Ashley all the way back in kindergarten. She always gave me her cookies at snack time. All the other girls wanted to beat me up. I was a lot shorter then. So I guess it was really her niceness that got to me first. And she's still like that. She always has time to listen to people. Well, almost always. She's been sort of busy lately, and sometimes I think . . . well, never mind that.

MARY-KATE: Is there anything that you think could make your relationship with Ashley even more perfect?

AARON: Yeah, of course. If Ashley could loosen up a little, it would make things really great. I mean, I totally admire her for being so organized. But she's a bit of a control freak, you know? (LAUGHS.) It makes it hard for me to be spontaneous and romantic when she's always making all our plans in advance. And I *want* to be romantic with her. All I have to do is look at her and I know I totally lucked out. . . .

Interview Number Three: Malcolm Freeman

MARY-KATE: Malcolm, what first attracted you to Sophie?

MALCOLM: Hey, do I really have to answer that? I don't think it's anybody's business.

MARY-KATE: Malcolm, you promised.

MALCOLM: Okay, okay. What was the question again?

MARY-KATE: What first attracted you to Sophie?

MALCOLM: Oh. Her breath. No. The fact that she had heard of *Attack of the Killer Tomatoes!* I guess. I mean, how many kids these days know that movie? A classic. That's when I knew Sophie had great taste. And my nosebleeds never gross her out. I mean, she doesn't barf or anything. She just makes me hold my head back and stuff. Look, you know me, Mary-Kate. I'm not the easiest person in the world. Well, Sophie's willing to put up with that. She sees below the surface, to who I really am inside—a real animal. A Komodo dragon, actually.

So many people are losers, you know? Like only caring about looking good and being popular. Sophie doesn't care about that stuff. Plus she reads everything. I guess it's because of her job at the bookstore. She knows a lot about the stuff I'm into. So I don't have to explain everything to her all the time . . . like I do to you and your sister!

Interview Number Four: Sophie Curtis

MARY-KATE: Much as we all love him, Malcolm can't be the easiest person to go out with.

SOPHIE: That's true. He's not your average guy. He drives me nuts sometimes. He gets focused on the weirdest stuff. Like when he got that boa constrictor. Ick. I can't believe he actually had to feed it live mice! I don't even want to think about it! And you've got to admit that anybody whose favorite animal is a Komodo dragon has got to be a little twisted. I mean, their bites are, like, totally poisonous. And they actually throw up the bones and teeth of their victims! It's disgusting. Plus his taste in movies is really extreme. Sometimes when he chooses a movie for us to see, I walk out in the middle. I just can't take it. But even when we disagree about stuff like that, he can be so sweet and caring. And he's honest. He always tells me the truth—even sometimes when I don't want to hear it. And he's his own person. Malcolm won't change for anyone. I mean, I keep wishing he'd throw out that ratty pair of green pants. They are truly gross. . . .

Interview Number Five: Lauren Glazer

MARY-KATE: Lauren, do you think you and Ben are the perfect couple?

LAUREN: Perfect—who knows? But things are pretty great. I know we're meant to be together. I felt so terrible when we broke up that time. And Ben is so sweet to me. He even sings love songs along with the radio when we go out. Don't print that, okay? I don't want to embarrass him or anything. I mean, he has a terrible voice, but it's the thought that counts, don't you think?

MARY-KATE: So—what do you like most about Ben?

LAUREN: Um . . . his sense of humor. Sometimes he makes me laugh so hard that my stomach actually hurts.

MARY-KATE: Is there anything you'd change about Ben?

LAUREN: Uh . . . his sense of humor! (LAUGHS.) No, I didn't mean that. Maybe I'd want him to be a little more serious about some stuff sometimes. And he could absolutely use a new wardrobe! But I'm really nuts about him. When I'm with Ben, no matter what happens, somehow I know things will turn out fine. So I guess I'd only change little things about him.

Interview Number Six: Ben Jones

MARY-KATE: Tell me about Lauren. What do you like best about her?

BEN: Her low expectations of a boyfriend. Only kidding! Lauren is the best person I know. She takes in stray animals. She looks for the bright side of everything. She's always pointing out the good in people. Even me. Hmm. Now that I think about it, she must be nuts!

MARY-KATE: So, are you the perfect couple?

BEN: The perfect couple? Sounds like Barbie and Ken or something. I don't think there is a perfect couple. It'd probably be boring if there were. The thing is, Lauren is the nicest girl I know. But I wonder if there can be such a thing as too nice. I mean, she never, ever gets mad at me! It's hard to believe that anyone can be that sweet. Sometimes it even makes me a little uncomfortable. I don't know. On the other hand, most of the time I love her, I guess. I'm not sure I've ever even told her that. But I seriously do. . . .

End of transcript

chapter seven

"Hey, Lauren. Would you hold these for a second?"

Lauren reached for the stack of Valentine's Day dance posters in my arms. "Sure, Ashley. Just give them here."

"Thanks!" I reached up and pulled down an old New Year's Eve party poster. Then I took one of the Valentine's Day posters and started taping it up next to the gym door. There was a boys' gym class in progress, and I could hear the muffled shouts of guys and the *thunk* of balls hitting the polished wood floor. A whistle blew.

Brittany came up behind me. She looked at the poster, her head tilted to one side.

"A little higher on the right, Ashley. A bit more. No, a bit less. Yeah, that's good."

"Thanks, Britt." I put the last piece of tape in place.

"Everybody is so psyched about having Angel at the dance," Brittany said as we headed down the hall. "I can't believe you got her to come. You two are amazing!"

"Not me," said Lauren. "All the credit belongs to Ashley. I never would have had the nerve to talk to Angel myself."

"That's not true," I said. "Besides, I couldn't have done it without you. I needed your support to work up the courage to open my mouth."

We walked under a big banner that hung in the hallway near the lunchroom. SPEND VALENTINE'S DAY IN HEAVEN! it read. COME TO THE BAYSIDE HIGH VALENTINE'S DAY DANCE AND SEE AN ANGEL SING!

Not bad, I thought. Angel was definitely the biggest star ever to perform at Bayside. This year's dance was going to be the best in the history of the school!

The bell rang. "Oops," said Brittany. "Gotta run. French class. Madame Berthold." She made a face. "*Au revoir!*" She gave a wave and dashed off.

"Me, too," Lauren said. "I'm sorry, Ashley. I have chemistry lab." She handed me the rest of the posters.

"No problem," I said. "I've got a free period, so I'll just finish hanging these up. See you later."

Lauren took off down the hall. I looked around to see if there were any empty spaces on the walls where I could put up other posters. I saw one above the water fountain.

I took a poster and put the rest down on the black-and-white tiled floor. Then I stood on tiptoe and started to tape the poster in place. I had just finished with the two top corners when someone came up behind me.

I figured whoever it was wanted to get to the water fountain, so I tried to move aside. But before I could get out of the way, somebody kissed me on the cheek.

I turned, knowing exactly who it was. "You!" I said happily. "Have you got a free period, too?"

"Uh-huh." Aaron grinned at me. He pointed at the poster. "Hard at work, I see."

"Want to join the crew?"

With Aaron's help, I finished putting up the poster. Then I picked up the rest of them and headed down the hall.

"Let me take those," Aaron offered.

"That's okay. You're carrying all your books. I can manage."

"So." Aaron smiled down at me. "What's up?"

"Oh, nothing much," I said. "Except that Mr. Trask has dumped an incredible amount of homework on us for over the weekend."

"That's too bad," Aaron said, "because I was just about to ask you what you were doing

Saturday night. I thought we could go to a movie or something."

"Oh, Aaron, I'm totally sorry. But Lauren and Brittany and I are going shopping on Saturday to get the stuff we need to make the decorations for the dance. And we're going to head to Click afterward to do some more planning."

"Ashley, the dance is almost a month away!" Aaron said.

"I know that. But people buy their holiday decorations so early. We want to make sure that we have everything we need in plenty of time." I thought for a moment. "How about Friday night? I'm free then. I can do my homework on Saturday night and Sunday, so we could go out on Friday."

Aaron shook his head. "That won't work. I have to go to my aunt's for dinner. It's my uncle's birthday."

"How about—" I never came up with another suggestion because just then a group of kids came up to us.

"Hey, Ashley," said Melanie. She wore a cute orange and pink dress that set off her straight, shiny black hair, and her brown eyes glowed. "You really did it this time. Angel at Bayside High! What are you wearing? My dad got me the most gorgeous dress from Paris. I can't wait for you to see it!"

Paula Cooper nodded, her long red braids bobbing. "You are incredible, Ashley. I can't even get tickets to the next Angel concert, and you scored her for our school. How great is that?"

Danielle Bloom shook her strawberry blond hair out of her eyes. "Even my mom is impressed. Angel is superhot right now. Mom says she met Angel once at an Actor's Fund benefit before Angel got so famous and that she was really sweet."

I nodded. "She still is. Lauren and I met her at a CD signing, and she was totally cool."

"What was she wearing?" Melanie wanted to know.

"A really cute red miniskirt with a black tank top," I told her. "And she had this beautiful silver necklace with red stones—maybe garnets—"

"Sounds fantastic," said Melanie. "So, I know you and Aaron must be going to the dance together. But who's taking Mary-Kate? Is she dating anybody?"

Aaron. I suddenly remembered Aaron.

I looked around for him, but he was gone. When had he disappeared? I was so involved in talking about the dance that I hadn't even noticed.

Oh, well, I thought. *I'll catch him later at lunch.*

"Mary-Kate's not dating anyone right now," I said, turning back to my friends. "She's been so busy at *Girlz* magazine that I hardly ever see her."

"I forgot she got that job." Melanie's eyes lit up. "I wonder if she's getting a chance to try on any of the hot new fashions they photograph. They get stuff *months* before it reaches the stores! Mary-Kate is so lucky. All those beautiful clothes. She must be thrilled!"

"What she's really thrilled about is that she might get an article published in the February issue," I said. "She interviewed me and Aaron for it."

"That is too cool!" said Paula. "What's it about?"

"The perfect couple," I told her.

"That definitely describes you and Aaron," said Danielle.

I smiled. But deep down I was starting to have doubts. There was something about the way Aaron had been behaving lately. Like just now. He left without even saying good-bye. And wouldn't the "perfect couple" be seeing more of one another? *How perfect were we really?* I wondered.

❁

C.K. frowned. She flipped back to the first page of my article and read through it one more time.

I sat in front of her desk, watching her. C.K. didn't like what I had written. I could tell. Liam was going to get published, and I wasn't. I felt as though I had swallowed a big rock and it was sitting in my chest.

C.K. finally put down the pages and looked up at me.

"It's well written, Mary-Kate," she said. She took off her glasses and rubbed the bridge of her

58

nose. "But we need *great*. The stuff we print in *Girlz* has to really *grab* our readers. There's so much that demands their attention—homework, friends, TV, movies, music. The minute you lose them, they're out the door. You've got some interesting ideas here. But everybody comes off bland, boring. You've got to spice it up more."

I took a deep breath. She didn't totally hate it. And I knew she was right. I'd had a feeling there was something wrong with the article, but I didn't know what it was.

I nodded. "I can make it more interesting, C.K. I know I can."

"Good." C.K. handed the article back to me. "I'm depending on you and Liam to give me something I can use, Mary-Kate. I want you to E-mail me your second draft by Monday. If it's good, I'll use both yours and Liam's. Don't let me down."

Then, in typical C.K. fashion, she picked up the phone, punched in a number, and waved me out of her office.

Well, at least she wants me to try again! I thought as I closed the door behind me. I turned and almost jumped a foot. Liam was standing a few inches away from me. Had he heard what C.K. said about my article? I could feel my face getting hot.

"Hey, Mary-Kate," Liam said. "Are you okay?"

"Why shouldn't I be okay?" I said.

Liam gestured to C.K.'s office. "She can be a little rough."

"Not on me," I said. Then I turned and walked down the hall.

Liam followed me. "Well, if there's anything I can do—" he began.

"I'll be sure to ask you," I said. "Absolutely."

Liam grinned. "Good. I've been getting the feeling that you've been a little . . . well, annoyed with me lately."

"Annoyed? Why should I be annoyed?" I snapped. "What could possibly make me annoyed?"

Liam put his hands up in the air. "Look, I'm sorry. I didn't mean to bug you." He turned and headed down the hallway. "I'll see you later, okay?" he said over his shoulder. Then he was gone.

Bug me? I guess you could call it that. It felt as if he had been trying to get on the good side of everyone in the office—at my expense—ever since he started at *Girlz*.

I frowned. Jealousy was not helpful. Whatever Liam was trying to do shouldn't matter to me one bit. I was going to rewrite my article so that it was anything but boring. C.K. was going to love it. Okay, maybe both Liam's article and mine would be published in the February issue of *Girlz*.

But mine was going to be better!

On Friday night I reread the transcripts of my interviews over and over again. Then I listened to the tapes and made some more notes.

I was beginning to see how I could make the article a lot more interesting—by putting in some of the stuff I'd left out when I wrote the first draft.

For example, Malcolm probably had no idea about how grossed out Sophie really was about some of the stuff he liked. Like that Komodo dragon thing. Yuck! He really ought to know. After all, isn't honesty the best policy? That's what everyone always says. So maybe I'd be helping everyone if each person knew what the other really thought.

I nodded slowly to myself. *Yes,* I thought. *If I just rework some of these answers, I can make the article more interesting.* And C.K. would like it, I was sure.

I turned on the computer and got to work.

A few hours later Ashley poked her head around my door. "Hey, Mary-Kate! Don't tell me you're doing homework on a Friday night?"

I grinned at my sister and leaned back in my chair. "This isn't homework. I'm working on my article."

She came into my room and plunked down on my bed. "Between your job and the dance, I feel like I never see you."

"I know." I stretched. "And don't forget Aaron. Did you guys go out tonight?"

Ashley frowned. "No. He had to go over to his uncle's for dinner or something. I was with Britt and Lauren at Click."

"Is there anything wrong between you and Aaron?" I asked.

"No. Yes. I'm not sure," Ashley answered. "I think everything's fine. It's probably just my imagination. I'm working so hard on the dance that there's just not enough time for us to be together."

"I'm actually glad I'm not dating anyone at the moment," I said. "Life is just too complicated."

Ashley got up. "I know what you mean," she said, coming over to stand behind me. "So. Can I take a look at the article?"

I glanced at my computer. My screen-saver was on. It was a picture of me and Ashley when we were five, dressed in our Halloween costumes. Ashley was a princess in a flowing pink gown. I was a witch, complete with green makeup and pointy black hat.

"Not right now," I said quickly. "I want to keep the whole thing a secret until it's published. Then you can read it in the actual magazine."

"Okay, Mary-Kate," Ashley said. "Whatever you say." She headed for the door.

"'Night, Ashley. Love you," I said.

"Love you, too, Mary-Kate." Ashley blew me a kiss and left the room, closing the door behind her.

I went back to work.

The next thing I knew, it was after one in the morning. I sat back and yawned. The article was done!

I read it over. I fixed some typos and added a sentence or two. Finally I changed all the names in the article to fake ones. It wouldn't be right to use my friends' real names! Then I reread it. It was looking pretty good.

I stared at the screen.

Should I read it one more time over the weekend and give it to C.K. on Monday?

I closed my eyes for a moment. Maybe it would be better to hold on to it. I wasn't completely sure about some of the stuff I had added. . . .

No. I opened my eyes. I had done a good job. I knew it. And I also knew that C.K. liked people who got their articles in before deadline—like Liam. My best move would be to E-mail it to C.K. right now. She'd be impressed that I'd gotten it in so quickly. At least, I hoped she would be.

I wrote her a short message.

C.K.: I just finished my second draft. Hope it works better this time. Mary-Kate

Then I attached the article.

I took a deep breath and pressed SEND.

Now it was up to C.K. If she liked it, it would be published in a national magazine! If not . . . well, I'd worry about that tomorrow.

"Stop it!" I was furious. "Liam, cut it out now!"

Liam was laughing at me. Then C.K. came over and stood right in front of me. "I hated the article," she said, poking me with her pencil. "I hated it!"

"But I thought—" I didn't understand. Why did she hate my article?

I opened my eyes. Sunlight streamed in through the window.

Whew! I thought. *It was only a dream!*

I rolled out of bed and looked at the clock. It was exactly 11:14 A.M. I wondered if CK had read the article by now. *She probably doesn't even look at her E-mail over the weekend,* I thought. But I knew she did.

Maybe she'd sent me an E-mail, just to say she'd received mine. I couldn't resist. I turned on my computer. And sure enough, I had a message from her.

My hand shook a little as I double-clicked on it. I read it quickly.

Mary-Kate: Nice job. Needs slight editing, but I'll handle. Congratulations—it's in the magazine. Am using Liam's article, too. You both did good. C.K.

I sat there staring at the E-mail. I could hardly believe it. I was going to be published in *Girlz* magazine!

chapter eight

A few weeks later, on a Tuesday afternoon, I arrived at the *Girlz* offices and saw a messenger stacking ten large cardboard boxes beside Lacey's desk.

"Are those the February issues?" I asked. I'd been waiting for this moment ever since I'd gotten C.K.'s E-mail. I couldn't believe the issues were here so fast—and that my Valentine's Day article was inside every single one of them! I had to remind myself that it was unprofessional to jump up and down with excitement.

"Yup." Lacey smiled and grabbed a pair of scissors. "C.K. is usually the first person to see them. But since your article is in there, let's sneak a peek, okay?"

"Okay?" I echoed. "I'm going to die of suspense if we don't!"

"Ta-da!" she sang out, neatly cutting the tape that sealed one of the boxes. "Go ahead, Mary-Kate," she said. "Open it up."

Slowly I turned back the cardboard flaps. The February issue sat there, a picture of Angel Velasquez on the cover. Ashley was thrilled when I told her Angel was being featured. Somehow it seemed like a good sign for both of us.

I quickly scanned the cover lines. There it was—my article, listed at the top of the cover, above the logo. LOVE AND KISSES! ARE YOU THE PERFECT COUPLE? WIN A PERFECT DATE . . . . PAGE 72.

I flipped to page seventy-two. My byline stared up at me in black and white: *by Mary-Kate Olsen.* My palms actually got sweaty. The articles and pictures I published on the school Website were seen only by students and people with the password. But this article was going to be read by millions all over the country!

"Good job, M.K.," a voice behind me said. I turned around. C.K. was standing there. She was actually smiling!

"I remember how it felt to see my name in print for the first time," she said. "Enjoy it. And when you're done, we need some coffee back there." She turned and went into her office.

Trust C.K. to bring me back to earth just when I was flying high. Still, I couldn't help grinning.

"Congratulations, Mary-Kate." Lacey gave me a quick hug. "The article looks great. You should be very proud."

"I am," I said. "Thanks, Lacey."

It wasn't until I was grinding the espresso beans that I realized something: C.K. had called me M.K.

I had arrived!

Of course, the first thing I did when I sat down at my desk—after my coffee chores—was read my article. The funny thing is, it seemed a little . . . different in print. But I couldn't say why. I shook my head and turned to Liam's article. I read it quickly. I had to admit, he was a terrific writer.

Later that afternoon, while I was doing some on-line research for C.K., Liam stopped by my desk.

"Hey, Mary-Kate," he said. "I read your article. Your writing's really good. I don't know about the title, though. Those couples aren't exactly perfect."

"That's the point," I said. "Everyone who knows them thinks they're perfect, and they're all really happy with each other, *but* . . ."

"True." He nodded. "Actually, I'm glad C.K. decided to publish both our pieces."

"Me, too," I admitted. "I liked your article a lot."

Liam smiled. "Glad you approve. Anyway, I'll see you later. Congratulations."

After Liam left, I felt a little confused. Just when I thought Liam was only out for himself, he acted really nice. Like a friend. I didn't get it.

I shook myself. Who cared? Right now I wanted to share my article with my real friends—the six friends I had written about! Suddenly I knew what to do. I'd messenger each of them an advance copy of the magazine, complete with a thank-you note.

❁

At home that night I sat at my desk and pulled out my extra-special turquoise-blue stationery.

Dear Ashley, I wrote. *Not only are you a perfect sister—you're a perfect best friend! And now you're part of a perfect couple—in print! Here's the issue of* Girlz *magazine with my article in it. Thanks so much for letting me interview you. Love, hugs, and kisses, Mary-Kate.*

I slipped the letter and a copy of the magazine into a mailing envelope and sealed it. Taking out a second piece of stationery, I started on Aaron's letter. I couldn't wait for everyone to see my article. I knew they were all going to love it!

My jaw dropped open as I stared at the glossy pages of *Girlz* magazine. "I can't believe Mary-Kate wrote that!"

Lauren, Brittany, and I were sitting on a sofa at Click reading Mary-Kate's article.

"Listen to this," I said. "Mary-Kate called me 'Abby' in the article, and she called Aaron 'Alex.'

Here's what Alex has to say about Abby." I read aloud: " 'If Abby could loosen up a little, it would make things really great. I mean, she's a bit of a control freak, you know?' " I stopped reading and took a shaky breath. "I never knew Aaron felt that way about me."

"It is pretty harsh," Brittany admitted.

"How about Ben?" Lauren demanded. Her freckles stood out against her pale cheeks. "This is what he said about me: 'She's the nicest girl I know. But I wonder if there can be such a thing as too nice. Sometimes it makes me really uncomfortable.' " Lauren was almost in tears. "What does Ben want me to do—be mean? Yell at him?"

"I'm sure he didn't mean it that way," I said, giving Lauren a quick hug. I read on. "You know," I said slowly. "It's not like Mary-Kate made anything up. I said everything she wrote here. But she changed it somehow."

"Exactly," Lauren agreed. "We all sound almost . . . well . . . mean! You'd think none of us actually liked each other."

When I got to the part where "Abby"—that was me—talked about "Alex"—that was Aaron—my throat got tight. "Oh, no," I moaned. "How could she write this? Aaron's going to hate me."

"That's crazy," Brittany said at once. "Aaron's completely wild about you."

"But this article makes it sound like I think he's—"

A shadow fell over the magazine. I looked up and froze. There, standing in front of me, carrying his very own copy of *Girlz*, was Aaron. He did not look wild about me.

"Thanks a lot, Ashley," he said. "I really appreciate your making me sound like a total wimp."

"Aaron, that's not what I meant at all!" I cried. "Besides, how about what you said about me? Do you really think I'm a . . . a control freak?"

Aaron's blue eyes were icy. "Well, we always seem to end up at the places *you* want to go to, doing the things *you* want to do. What do *you* think?"

That hurt so much, I could barely breathe. But I wasn't going to let Aaron know that. I kept my voice calm as I said, "Well, I'm glad you made that so clear. If I'd known you felt that way about me, I never would have gone out with you in the first place."

"Maybe I shouldn't have asked you out in the first place," Aaron shot back.

My eyes filled with tears. Did Aaron really mean that? And if he didn't, why had he said those terrible things about me?

All four of us jerked around at the sound of a loud banging. It was coming from the coffee bar.

"I knew it!" It was Malcolm. He was banging his head on the counter, a copy of *Girlz* beside him. "Sophie hates me. Our relationship was doomed from the start!"

Brittany got up and went over to him. "Malcolm, take it easy, okay?" she said. "I know Sophie likes you. She's told me so herself. I think you're way overreacting."

Malcolm shook his head. "Listen to this! This is what she thinks of me." He started to read. "'You've got to admit that anybody whose favorite animal is a Komodo dragon has got to be a little twisted. I mean, they actually throw up the bones and teeth of their victims! It's pretty disgusting.'" Malcolm groaned. "She thinks I'm disgusting!"

Brittany shook her head impatiently. "Oh, please, Malcolm. Sophie thinks Komodo dragons are disgusting, not you."

But Malcolm wasn't listening. He picked up his copy of *Girlz* and stuffed it into a trash can. "My life is over. Sophie hates me! And no one else will ever go out with me again. What am I going to do?"

"I don't know," Brittany said. "But if I were you, I'd call Sophie right away." She turned to me. "And, Ashley? I think you should talk to your sister—the sooner the better."

I knew Brittany was right. I just didn't know what I was going to say to Mary-Kate.

On Wednesday afternoon I took a little detour on my way to the magazine office. I couldn't resist. I had to know what my friends thought of their advance copies. So I went to Click.

Sure enough, Ashley and Lauren were sitting at a table. Ashley had her copy of *Girlz* in her hands. Aaron stood over her, holding his own copy. Brittany was near the coffee bar, talking to Malcolm.

All five of them looked up as I came through the door.

"Hey, guys!" I said brightly. "What did you all think of the article?"

I expected Ashley to rush over and congratulate me. I expected everyone to be excited and happy. I expected wrong.

Ashley looked at me as if she didn't quite recognize me. "I don't get it, Mary-Kate," she said slowly. "What you wrote in the article—it's just not right. I mean, it may be what we said, but it's not what we *meant*. Is this what you handed in, or did they change it in some way?"

"That must be it. That editor you work for must have changed it," Lauren said quickly. "Right, Mary-Kate? You didn't really write this, did you? I mean, I don't remember telling you this stuff. Not in the way it came out, anyway. And Ben. Ben doesn't really feel this way about me . . . does he?"

Aaron looked miserable. Malcolm didn't look at me at all.

"You didn't like the article?" I was stunned. I turned to Brittany. "They didn't like the article?"

"I think that's obvious," Brittany said.

"Like it?" Aaron shook his head. "You've got to be kidding, Mary-Kate." With that, he pushed past me and out the door.

I stood there like a stone, feeling a huge lump forming in my throat. Ashley didn't like the article. Lauren didn't like it. Aaron was actually mad at me. I looked over at Malcolm just as he buried his head in his hands. He obviously wasn't too thrilled. And I was pretty sure I wasn't going to be very popular with Sophie or Ben, either.

"I'm so sorry—" I started to say. But as I looked at Ashley and Lauren, the words died in my throat. *Sorry* clearly wouldn't cut it.

It didn't matter that I hadn't *meant* to hurt anyone. They *had* been hurt. I felt completely awful.

The magazine article was headed for newsstands everywhere. The damage was done.

What could I do to make things right? What could *anybody* do?

chapter nine

"Hi, sweetie." Mom looked at me from the hall-way as she slipped off her jacket. "What's up?"

"Nothing much," I told her. It was true. Nothing was up. Everything was down. Especially me.

I was camped out in front of the tube in the family room, downing a pint of mocha java ice cream and channel surfing. A copy of *Girlz* was spread out in front of me on the coffee table.

I pointed the remote at the TV. Reality show, reality show, rerun, rerun, news. Boring, boring, boring, boring, depressing. I ate another scoop of ice cream.

"No homework tonight?" Mom asked me.

"I finished it already."

She walked into the family room and looked at the television. "What's that?" she asked.

"A movie about a chimpanzee and a kid from outer space," I told her.

She sighed. Then she noticed the copy of *Girlz*. "Hey!" she said, picking it up and looking at the cover. "This is it! Your article! Congratulations!"

"Thanks."

Mom looked at me. Her eyes narrowed. Then she sat down next to me on the couch. Gently she took the remote out of my hands and turned off the TV.

"Okay, Mary-Kate," she said. "What's wrong?"

"Read the article," I told her.

She opened the magazine and started to read. I took a few more bites of ice cream. It was melting fast.

Mom finished the article at the same time I finished the carton. She put the magazine down in her lap.

"So, do *you* like it?" I asked. "No one else seems to. Especially—" Something caught in my throat and I coughed. "Ashley. She and Aaron are having a huge fight over it. Lauren is upset, and so is Malcolm. I'm afraid to talk to Sophie and Ben. Even Brittany thinks it stinks. And she isn't even in it!"

"Why do you think they don't like it?"

"Don't like it!" I almost laughed. "They hate it! And I don't know why! C.K. liked it. She thought it was great! And it's not as if I made any of it up. It's all on tape. I can play it for you if you want—"

Mom smiled. "You don't need to do that. I believe you." Then she just sat there looking at me.

The silence grew longer and longer. Mom sat, waiting. She always does this to me. And it always works.

"I really wanted to get published in *Girlz*," I said at last. "I wanted to beat out Liam. I wanted to make C.K. happy. What was so wrong about that?"

Mom didn't say anything. She just listened.

"I mean, Ashley should know," I went on. "When you're talking to a writer, everything you say is fair game. Writers have to shape things to make them interesting to readers. I only wrote what Ashley said. It's not like I lied or anything. . . ."

I stopped talking. That's when I knew.

I *had* stretched the truth.

It wasn't that I'd misquoted anyone. I was careful to use the exact words from the interviews. Some of them, anyway. I left out a lot of the nicer things my friends had said about each other. I wrote the article in a way that told the story I wanted to tell. The story C.K. wanted me to write. The story that would get me published.

"Oh, Mom!" I wailed. "What am I going to do?"

My mom gave me a quick hug. "Why don't you start by apologizing to your sister?" she suggested.

77

Talk about perfect timing. At that very moment Ashley walked into the family room. She froze when she saw me and Mom. She looked as if she'd been crying. Then, without a word, she turned and headed up the stairs.

I looked at Mom.

"Go on," she said, taking the empty ice cream carton out of my hands. "Talk to her."

I took the stairs two at a time. I reached Ashley's door just as she slammed it shut.

"Ashley," I called through the door. "Ashley, I've got to talk to you. I feel terrible. I didn't mean to write anything that would hurt you. You have to know that!"

No answer.

I tried again. "You're right. I used your words in the article, but they didn't come out the way you meant them. Especially what you said about Aaron and what he said about you."

Still *nada*.

"If you won't talk to me, at least talk to him," I pleaded. "I know you're mad at me, and I deserve it. But don't get angry at Aaron because of something I did."

The door stayed shut.

"Ashley," I went on, "I want to make it right. What can I do to help? Just tell me. I'll do anything at all. I'll go talk to Aaron if you want. Please don't shut me out!"

I tried turning the doorknob. It was unlocked. I waited for a moment. Then I pushed open the door.

Ashley lay on her bed with her head buried in her pillow, facing away from me. I went and sat down next to her.

"There's nothing you can do," Ashley said. Her voice was muffled. "Aaron and I broke up."

"You broke up?" I gasped. "You and Aaron? You didn't! I mean—you were the perfect couple!" I clapped a hand over my mouth. How completely stupid could I get?

"It's over," Ashley said. She raised her head from the pillow. Her face was stained with tears.

"Oh, Ashley!" I cried. "I'm so sorry. It's all my fault!"

"No, it isn't, Mary-Kate." Ashley grabbed a tissue from her bedside table and wiped her eyes. "Aaron started acting weird months ago. I think that deep down he really does believe that stuff he told you. And the Valentine's Day dance was so important to me, I guess I ignored all the signs. I was ignoring *him*." She sniffed. "When I wasn't bossing him around, that is."

"Wait a minute!" I said, getting an idea. "I may still have the original article. The one C.K. rejected. The one that has all the really sweet things Aaron said about—"

"Forget it," Ashley cut me off. "It's too late. Aaron and I are history. We were the ones with the problem, not you. You wrote a good article—good enough to get into the magazine. That was your job."

I shook my head to clear it. I couldn't believe what I was hearing. I was responsible for breaking up my sister and her boyfriend. And she was telling me I had just been doing my job!

What was going on here?

And, more important, what could I do to make it right?

chapter ten

The next afternoon I marched into the *Girlz* magazine offices with a plan. It wasn't much of a plan, but it was all I could come up with.

I was going to beg C.K. to let me print a follow-up to the article in the next issue—to tell the whole truth and nothing but. It wouldn't be published for another month, but at least it would set the record straight. And maybe it wouldn't be too late to get Ashley and Aaron back together.

"Is everything okay, Mary-Kate?" Lacey looked up as I came into the reception area. "You look a little blue."

"Nothing is okay." I sighed. "I'll tell you about it later. Right now I have to talk to C.K."

"Well, if there's anything I can do, just ask," Lacey said sympathetically.

"Thanks," I said, and I headed in to face the music.

C.K.'s office door was closed. I knocked. "Enter!" she called.

"M.K.!" C.K. was actually smiling. "Just the person I wanted to see. Look at this!" She pointed to a stack of letters on her desk. "And that's just the snail mail. We've already gotten E-mails from over a hundred readers. And they all liked your article."

"They did?"

"They did. In fact, they loved it," C.K. said. "Congratulations, M.K. I have a feeling you've got the makings of a top-notch reporter."

"Uh, thanks," I said. "But—"

The phone rang, and C.K. dove for it. "Hello?" she barked into the receiver. "Yeah? Good. Hold on a sec." She put a hand over the receiver. "Excuse me, M.K.," she said. "It's my vet. Fluffy hasn't been eating much lately. I think she has worms."

I nodded and walked out of her office. There was no point in staying. I couldn't ask C.K. to let me print a follow-up article now. I couldn't tell her I had pushed the article too far, that I had sort of exaggerated the whole thing. Not when she was so happy with it.

I went back to my desk feeling totally miserable.

So, I couldn't use the magazine to apologize to everyone. What *could* I do to help my sister and Aaron get back together? What could I do to make it up to my friends?

I sat at my desk, staring at the February issue with its big picture of Angel on the cover. And suddenly I realized something that made me feel even worse. Valentine's Day! I'd been so busy with my job that I hadn't really thought about it much. Ashley and Aaron had broken up less than two weeks before the dance!

Ashley had worked so hard to book Angel and to make the dance a big success. Now she'd have to go alone . . . if she went at all.

I put my head in my hands. I wanted Ashley to be happy. And if that meant getting her back together with Aaron, I'd have to figure out some way to do it.

But how?

"Ashley? Lauren? Brittany?" I turned to see Mrs. Walsh, Principal Needham's secretary, bustling into the gym. She had a worried look on her face.

"Oh, girls, I'm so glad you're here! I have some terrible news. I don't know how it could have happened. I'm so sorry! But it's not too late to change the date, I'm sure. And I'll do everything I can to help."

"What's the matter, Mrs. Walsh?" I asked, getting up from the floor and brushing off my skirt. Bits of red and pink crepe paper floated down around my feet. It was February fourth and we were busy making the Valentine's Day dance decorations.

"Your Valentine's Day dance, the one you're holding a week from Saturday—" Mrs. Walsh began. "I'm so sorry, girls, but you can't have it in the gym. Not on Saturday, the fifteenth. There's a gigantic Parents' Association fund-raiser scheduled for that night, and it's being held in the gym. The gym is the only place that's big enough. It should have been on my calendar, but the Parents' Association never told me, and the mayor is coming, so we can't change the date. I'm so sorry. You'll have to change the date of the dance."

I couldn't believe my ears. "Change the date of the dance when it's only eleven days away? Mrs. Walsh, we can't do that. We've invited—"

"You can have it on Friday," she broke in, trying to sound cheerful. "That would be okay, wouldn't it? Friday is actually Valentine's Day, after all."

As if breaking up with Aaron wasn't bad enough. Now the dance was turning into a disaster.

Lauren put a hand on my arm. "What are we going to do?" she asked worriedly.

I didn't have an answer. *Stop panicking and get it together, Ashley,* I told myself.

"I'll help in any way I can," Mrs. Walsh went on. "I feel terrible about this."

Mrs. Walsh is one of the nicest people at Bayside High. I couldn't stand seeing her so upset. "It's not your fault," I told her.

Brittany made a face at me, meaning, *Yes, it is!*

I ignored her and turned back to Mrs. Walsh. "It's okay, really. Things happen. I just wish they weren't happening to me right now."

Lauren smiled at Mrs. Walsh. "Maybe we *could* change it."

"Look," Brittany said, deciding to be helpful. "We can handle it. For one thing, we can put an announcement on the school Website."

"And I can help you girls take down the old posters and put new ones up," Mrs. Walsh added.

I took a deep breath. There was a lot of work to be done.

"First I have to contact Angel," I said decisively. I put a hand on Mrs. Walsh's arm. "Don't worry. We'll make it happen."

"I'll go talk to Ms. Barbour about the Website," Brittany said. "I'm sure we can get something up right away."

"And I'll start taking down the posters, dear," Mrs. Walsh said.

"Hold on." I stopped her. "It might be better to leave them up. We can cross out the old date and write in the new one. Lauren, why don't you start on that? If you use a red marker, people will notice."

"Got it," Lauren said. "I'll get started now."

Lauren headed out of the gym. Mrs. Walsh followed her, offering to supply the red markers.

I pulled out my cell phone. I didn't even have to punch in Angel's number. I had put it on speed dial.

As I listened to her phone ring, I tried to feel confident. But deep down I was very, very worried. If Angel couldn't perform on Friday, we had a big problem on our hands. It was probably too late to get anyone else. And a dance without a band is no dance at all. The whole thing would be a complete dud!

Somehow I'd have to pull it all together. I'd find Angel, and I'd make sure she could perform on Friday. If she had a problem with that, I'd figure out a way to solve it.

Because if I didn't, this was definitely going to be the worst Valentine's Day of my life.

chapter eleven

"Oh, Lacey, I just don't know what to do!"

It was Friday afternoon, a week before Valentine's Day. Viv was out of town, and Lacey and I were holed up in her office. Head shots of gorgeous models hung everywhere. Aside from that, Viv's office was extremely neat. A polished oak desk sat in front of the window. Sleek gray file cabinets stood against the walls. There wasn't a loose piece of paper to be seen anywhere.

I put my feet up on the desk and stared at my shoes. "I feel like a creep," I said glumly. "I've got to figure out some way to help my sister."

Lacey's green eyes were sympathetic. "You'll think of something," she said.

"I'm not so sure," I told her. "It's not like I can get Ashley and Aaron stranded on a beautiful desert island somewhere, complete with palm trees and moonlight. I mean, I can't even get them to *talk* to one another. Believe me, I've tried!"

Lacey nodded. "It's too bad," she said. "Especially since everyone else really loves the article."

It was weird but true. Everybody *did* love the article—everybody but me, my best friends, and my sister. I glanced at a copy of the magazine that was sitting on Viv's desk. Then I stopped short.

"Hey, Lacey," I said. "Look at this."

"Look at what?"

"Here," I said. "On the cover. Liam's article."

"I know," Lacey said. "I read it. In fact, I used one of his ideas on my boyfriend. He really liked it."

"That's it!" I was starting to get excited. "What if I got Aaron the perfect present and sent it to him, complete with a really romantic note—from Ashley? And I got her something really terrific and sent it to her with a romantic note from Aaron?"

"It could be difficult to pull off," Lacey warned me. Her eyes sparkled with mischief. "But it just might work."

"It could be perfect!" I said, getting really excited. "If each of them got this great gift and thought the other one sent it, wouldn't they realize how much they still care for each other? Wouldn't they at least have to call to say thank you? And once they started talking, wouldn't they be able to patch things up?"

"Sounds definitely do-able," Lacey said.

"And I could do the same thing for Lauren and Ben and Malcolm and Sophie," I went on. "Though I can't imagine what the perfect gift for Malcolm would be. He has the weirdest taste!"

"Mary-Kate Olsen plays Cupid!" Lacey said.

"And what better time to play Cupid than around Valentine's Day?" I asked. "Maybe if I work fast, I can get everyone back together before the dance."

"That's fast, all right." Lacey opened the magazine and turned to Liam's article. "Let's take a look and see if Liam has any good ideas for you," she said. "Now what would Ashley get Aaron for Valentine's Day?"

We started to read.

I picked up the phone and hit REDIAL one more time. The phone rang and rang. When Angel's answering machine came on, I hung up.

I was in megapanic. I'd been calling Angel nonstop for four days now, and I kept getting a recording. And she wasn't calling back!

I rolled over onto my back on the sofa and stared at the ceiling. The sound of the TV in the family room got a little louder. There must be a commercial on. Yes, someone was saying something about toothpaste. *I wish getting whiter teeth was my biggest problem,* I thought, putting a throw pillow over my head.

"Any luck?" Dad asked, coming into the living room.

"Not yet," I groaned. "Where could Angel be?"

"She's a star, sweetie," Dad said, sitting down next to me and ruffling my hair. "She could be in Morocco for all we know."

"Did you hear from Mr. D'Andrea yet?"

"Not yet," Dad said. "But I'm sure he'll call me when he gets the message."

I jumped up and started pacing. "What is it with these people?" I asked. "Don't they ever stay home?"

Dad shook his head. "It's that kind of business, Ashley. Try to be patient. I'm sure someone will call soon."

Just then Mary-Kate walked in the front door. "Hey, Ashley," she said, dropping her backpack onto a chair and coming over to the couch. "Hi, Dad."

"Hi, Mary-Kate," said Dad, giving her a kiss. Then he diplomatically left the room.

"What's up?" Mary-Kate asked me. She perched on the arm of the couch.

"As if you didn't know," I said. Then I caught myself. "I'm sorry, Mary-Kate. That came out wrong. I'm still upset about Aaron, but that's not the problem right now. It's the dance."

"Don't worry," Mary-Kate said. "You guys have done an amazing job. Everybody in school knows about the date change."

"The problem is, Angel doesn't," I told her. "I've been calling for days, and I can't reach her. And if I can't reach her, I can't tell her what's happening. Plus I don't even know if she can make it on Friday. The whole thing is turning into a disaster of major proportions."

Mary-Kate slumped down next to me. She sat there for a second, lost in thought. Then she looked up. "I'll call Barb Weisz first thing in the morning," she said.

"Who's Barb Weisz?" I asked.

"She handles advertising and publicity at *Girlz*. She keeps track of everyone and everything. If anyone knows where Angel is, she will. And if she doesn't, maybe C.K. will have some ideas."

"Do you think?" I said, sitting up.

"We've got nothing to lose," Mary-Kate said.

"You're right." I sighed. "I sure hope someone at *Girlz* knows where Angel is. Because if they don't, our Valentine's Day dance is doomed!"

chapter twelve

"So when will you get the information?" Brittany asked Mary-Kate as we all walked to class on Monday morning.

"Barb usually gets in at about ten," Mary-Kate told her. "I've already left two messages with my friend Lacey—she's the receptionist at *Girlz*. I'm going to start calling at ten sharp. We should know pretty soon."

Just then I spotted Aaron out of the corner of my eye. He was standing at his locker talking to some of the guys.

My heart lurched. Seeing him still gave me goose bumps. I missed him a lot.

"I wonder if he misses me at all," I said aloud.

Brittany put a hand on my arm. "Of course he misses you," she said. "Don't be silly."

I glanced over at Aaron again. I thought he was staring at me, but he looked away as soon as he caught my eye. I shook my head. "We're not even talking. It's just hopeless."

"Ashley, it's not hopeless," Mary-Kate said. "I told you. The stuff in the article . . . well, it was exaggerated. And it left out all the sweet stuff he said. I don't think Aaron really meant the stuff that hurt you. I mean, I think you two are fighting about nothing. Well, maybe not nothing, but certainly not the big deal it seems to be."

I knew Mary-Kate was trying to help. No matter what she said, though, if felt like a pretty big deal to me. But as I looked over at Aaron again, I suddenly didn't care. I decided at that moment that I was going to talk to him. And the sooner the better, before I got cold feet. I wasn't going to let my pride stand in the way of our getting back together. I crossed my fingers. If only Mary-Kate was right, and there really was a chance . . .

I moved toward his locker. As I did, the group of guys broke up and started to move down the hall.

Aaron walked along with them—but not before he looked right at me.

I thought he was going to stop. I was sure of it. But then he looked away and kept right on going.

I stopped short. My throat closed up. It was clear that Aaron didn't even want to look at me.

Well, I'd simply have to figure out how to change that.

I wanted Aaron back. Whatever Mary-Kate had written, none of it mattered. I knew Aaron. I cared for him. And I knew he cared for me.

I just had to figure out how to remind him of that fact.

Things would be okay. They had to be.

So why did I feel so totally lousy?

✿

"Hey, Mary-Kate." Lacey looked up at me and smiled. "It's Monday afternoon. You're not supposed to work today. What are you doing here?"

"Trying to help Ashley," I told her. "Is Barb in?"

"I think so." Lacey studied the buttons on her phone. "Yup. Her line is busy, so she has to be in her office."

"I'll wait outside her door," I said. "Wish me luck."

"Good luck!" Lacey said.

She buzzed me in, and I raced down the hall to Barb's office. Her door was open. I looked in. It sounded as if her call was just winding up.

"Okay, I'll get right on it," she said into the phone. "Bye." She hung up, then waved at me to come in and sit down.

"Mary-Kate, I'm sorry," she said. "I just got your messages. I've been out with clients all day, and I had my cell phone turned off. What can I do for you?"

"I was wondering if you knew where Angel Velasquez might be," I asked her. "She's supposed to sing at our Valentine's Day dance this Saturday. My sister arranged it. But there's been a change in plans, and we can't reach her."

"Angel? At a high school dance?" Barb whistled. "If your sister ever wants a job, tell her to talk to me."

I smiled. "Thanks, I'll do that. Do you have any idea how we can contact Angel?"

"Wait a sec." Barb studied the tiny screen on her PDA. "I think I have her lawyer's number. Let me see. . . . Yeah, here it is."

Moments later Barb picked up the phone and dialed. I crossed my fingers.

"Hello, Ken? It's Barb Weisz. How are you? Great. Yeah, things are fine. Look, I need a favor. Do you know where Angel is these days?"

Barb listened for a second.

"Thanks, Ken. Yeah, I understand. Say hi to Bethie for me."

"I'm sorry, Mary-Kate," she said as she hung up the phone. "But he hasn't spoken with her in a few weeks."

My heart sank. "Thanks for trying, anyway."

I retreated to the coffee room to drown my sorrows in a quick cup of java. I had already spoken to C.K. on the phone that morning. She hadn't known how to reach Angel, either. Time was running out. I just had to figure out a way to help Ashley!

Just then Viv walked in.

"Any coffee left?" she asked, looking at the pot.

"Not much," I said gloomily. "I'll make some." I started filling the pot with water, then took out the coffee and a filter. "You wouldn't know anyone who knows Angel, the singer, would you?"

"No, I don't," Viv said. "Sorry, Mary-Kate. What's up?"

"She's supposed to sing at a Valentine's Day dance at my school, and there's been a change in plans, and we can't get ahold of her."

"Wish I could help," Viv said. "If I think of anything—"

"Thanks." I turned on the coffee machine. "This will be ready in a few minutes."

"I'll come back," Viv said. "Good luck with the Angel thing."

I sighed. "I'll need it."

Two seconds after Viv left the room, Liam walked in.

"What Angel thing?" he asked. "And what are you doing here? It's Monday."

"I could ask you the same question," I said.

"I had some work I couldn't get done on Thursday," he told me. "But we were talking about you and Angel. What's up?"

I shook my head. "It's hopeless. My sister got Angel to agree to sing at our Valentine's Day dance. But now the date of the dance is changing, and Ashley—my sister—can't reach Angel. She's getting desperate. The dance is this Friday night!"

"That's too bad," Liam. "Angel at Bayside High! What a story!"

I shook my head. Trust Liam to think of all the angles.

He stood there for a moment. "Have you tried Axel?" he asked finally. "After all, he's the music editor. If anyone knows where Angel is, he would."

"What a great idea!" I said. "I forgot all about Axel. I never see him in his office."

"He's there now," Liam said. "He usually checks in on Mondays. I just saw him. Let's go."

The two of us raced to Axel's office. Axel was just putting on his jacket.

"Sorry, kids—gotta fly. Muffy Bluestone is arriving at the airport at six. Traffic is going to be terrible."

"Axel," I said, "just give me five minutes. I've got to find Angel in a hurry."

"Angel?" Axel stopped. "How come?"

"It's a long story," I said. "But, believe me, it's important. Can you help?"

"Maybe," Axel said, sitting down at his desk. He picked up the phone and dialed a number.

"Hey, Louie! Axel here. How are you? Great! Great! Listen, do you have any idea where Angel is keeping herself these days? No? Yes? Good. I'll try her. Thanks. Let's get together for a drink when you're back in town. *Adios!*"

Axel hung up the phone and turned on his computer. He pressed some keys. Then he picked up the phone again and dialed another number.

"Veronica! It's Axel. How are you, darling? Yeah. You're kidding! Listen, sweetheart, do you know Angel's whereabouts? Louie said you might—yes? Uh-huh? Great. Thanks! See you at the Awards!"

Axel hung up the phone and wrote something down on a piece of paper. He handed it to me.

"When last sighted, Angel was at the Rancho La Paloma retreat. Heavy-duty yoga place. Serious business. No phones in the guest suites. Classes all day and all night. In Big Sur." He got up and grabbed his briefcase.

"Thanks, Axel!" I said. "You're the best!"

"Good luck," Axel said as he disappeared out the door. "Someday you'll have to tell me the whole story."

"Definitely!" I called after him. Then I turned to Liam.

"I owe you one," I said. "Thanks."

"Ask me to the dance," Liam said.

"What?" Was Liam asking me out?

"Ask me to the dance," he repeated. "I'd like to try to get an interview with Angel. Assuming you find her in time."

I should have known. On the other hand, Liam definitely deserved an invitation.

"Okay. You're invited," I told him. "You can pick me up at eight. Or you can just meet me there."

"I'll pick you up," Liam said.

"All right. It's this Friday, and my address is—"

"I know your address," Liam said. "I'll be there."

I nodded, then raced to my desk where I grabbed my phone and dialed Ashley's cell-phone number. As I waited for it to ring, I drummed my fingers on the desk. *Answer the phone, Ashley! I* said to myself. *Answer the phone! Where are you?*

I had to get Ashley the information about where Angel was right away.

If Ashley couldn't find Angel in a hurry, Liam wouldn't be going to the dance—and neither would I.

Because there wouldn't be a dance at all!

chapter thirteen

"Oh, please. You've got to get her a message! What? Don't tell me to take it easy! This is serious!"

I glanced at Brittany. She rolled her eyes.

The two of us were hanging out in Click when I got Mary-Kate's message. Now I was talking on my cell phone to some guy named Vardu. He worked at the yoga retreat where Angel was staying.

"I'm sorry," he said, "but we have an absolute policy. Our guests are treated with the utmost respect. They are here for rest and spiritual rejuvenation. There are no phone calls allowed. None. For any reason whatsoever. Unless it's a matter of life and death, of course."

"This *is* a matter of life and death," I said. "Mine!"

"You'll simply have to wait until Ms. Velasquez checks out," the man insisted.

"And when will that be?" I asked.

"Sorry. We cannot give out that information. Have a nice day." Vardu hung up.

I stared at the phone in disbelief.

"No luck?" Brittany asked me.

"Bad luck," I said as I closed the cover on my cell phone. "What am I going to do now?"

Brittany shook her head. "I honestly don't have a clue," she said. "Have you tried E-mailing Angel's agent?"

I shrugged. "I've tried everything. But I'll try again. It can't hurt."

One corner of Brittany's mouth lifted in a smile. "Good thing we happen to be in a cyber café."

"You're right!" I said, heading straight for one of the open computer stations. "Maybe we'll get through to him this time."

I sat down at the computer, typed another message to Mr. D'Andrea, and hit SEND. "Why do I have this feeling that Ms. Steele deletes these the second they show up?"

"Oh, Lauren told me about her," Brittany said, frowning. "You might be right."

"I don't know what else I can do to track down Angel," I admitted. "I've tried everything—cell phones, computers, leads from people in the business—and it's all led nowhere."

Brittany folded her arms and a stubborn look came into her dark eyes. "We can't give up," she said. "Things have been going downhill for a while now. Our luck has got to change. Somehow . . ."

❋

Poor Ashley, I thought as I drove to the mall on Tuesday afternoon. Since we'd worked on Monday, C.K. was giving both me and Liam Tuesday off. There were only three more days till the dance. I hoped Ashley would be able to find Angel in time.

In the meantime I was doing the only thing I could. I was heading off to play secret Cupid.

I finally figured out the perfect gifts for everyone. "Malcolm" was going to give Sophie a Monty Zweben CD of terrific love songs. "Sophie" was going to give Malcolm a first edition of his favorite book, *Weird New Jersey*.

Lauren was getting a bottle of her favorite perfume—Veronique—from "Ben," along with a bouquet of flowers. Ben was getting a CD mix of his favorite songs from "Lauren."

Aaron was getting a rubber ducky from "Ashley." That's because they had this sort of in-joke about ducks. When Aaron went out with Ashley for the first time, he told her about the crush he had on her when they were in kindergarten. He even remembered a

Thanksgiving play Ashley was in. She played the turkey but forgot her lines. So instead of "gobble, gobble," she said, "quack, quack, quack."

And for Ashley? That was the hardest. But "Aaron" had finally decided to give Ashley a beautiful photo of the two of them in a very special frame.

After searching through one major department store, three boutiques, two music stores, and three bookstores, I realized that this secret Cupid thing was going to be a little harder than I had expected. Lauren's perfume was easy, and I found a frame I liked pretty quickly, too. But Monty Zweben's CD was sold out everywhere. *Weird New Jersey* was nowhere to be found. And the only rubber ducky I could locate was really tiny and kind of cheap—nowhere near nice enough for "Ashley" to give to Aaron.

Just as I reached the doors of my fourth boutique, my cell phone rang. I reached into my bag and grabbed it.

"Hello?" I said.

"Mary-Kate? It's—" The line had so much static, I couldn't recognize the voice.

"Who is this?" I asked.

"Liam!"

I stopped short. Liam? Why was he calling me?

"Listen, Mary-Kate," he said. His voice broke up for a moment. "Meet me at Googly's. You know, the place right across the street from the office? I've got some information for you. It could be important." Then his voice broke up again.

"What is it?" I yelled into the phone. But the connection had gone dead.

I had no idea why Liam wanted to meet me, but I was too curious not to go. Anyway, Googly's was only about ten minutes from the mall. I turned around, raced to the parking lot, hopped into the Mustang, and was there in record time.

I parked in the lot behind Googly's and went in. A blast of air conditioning hit me, and I shivered. Liam was already sitting in a booth, coffee cup in hand. I slid in beside him.

"Sorry I had to drag you here," he said. "My cell phone battery was going dead, so there was no time to explain anything. I figured it would be easier for us to get together."

"So what's so important?" I asked him.

"This." He pulled out a piece of paper. "Remember how Axel mentioned that the guests at Rancho La Paloma had no phones? Well, this is the cell-phone number of a friend of my mom's. She happened to call my house about an hour ago, and I happened to pick up the phone. Mom couldn't talk, but I took a message. Guess where she was calling from?"

"Rancho La Paloma?" I said, stunned.

"Yup."

"How could she call your mom if they're not allowed to use the phone?" I asked.

"She never goes anywhere without her cell phone—rules or no rules," Liam said. He gave me a crooked smile. "When she told me where she was, it felt like fate. So I told her the problem. She says Ashley should call her A.S.A.P. She promised to find Angel if she had to walk all fifty miles of trails to do it!"

"Liam, I owe you another one," I told him. "Thanks so much. Can you wait just a minute? I've got to call Ashley right now!"

Liam nodded, and I went digging for my cell phone. Of course, that meant dumping my wallet, keys, and the shopping list for my secret Cupid mission on the table. Finally my cell phone emerged, and I called my sister.

Ashley didn't answer, so I left her a message. "Hey, Ashley. Mary-Kate. I've got a phone number at Rancho La Paloma for you to call." I read it out. "It belongs to a"—I looked at the paper again— "Mrs. Douglas Waterhouse. She knows all about what's going on. No time to explain. Just tell her who you are and mention the name Liam. She'll help you find Angel. Call her. Call me. Love you!"

I pressed END and looked up. Liam had my shopping list in his hand. He could certainly be nosy. He probably would make a great reporter someday.

I held out my hand for the list.

"What's this all about?" he asked, returning it to me.

So I told him all about playing Cupid. I wasn't going to at first, but he was a good listener. Another trait of a good reporter, now that I think about it.

"You've made some good choices," Liam said approvingly. "But it sounds like you're gonna need a little help if you want to get all those presents today. Why don't I come with you? I know a couple of used bookstores that might carry that New Jersey book. And I've been to every music store within a hundred miles of here."

"How about the rubber ducky?" I said. "Know any good squeaky-toy stores?"

"You'd be surprised," Liam said mysteriously. "I have a thing for rubber duckies myself." He laughed. "So, can I help?"

I looked at Liam across the table. This was really above and beyond the call of duty. "Yes!" I told him. "That would be great."

As we headed out to the parking lot, I kept sneaking glances at Liam. Finally I help myself. "Why are you being so nice?" I blurted out.

Liam actually looked a little hurt. "You don't think a lot of me, do you?" he asked.

"It's not that," I began, feeling confused. "It's just that you seemed so . . . well, competitive when I first met you. You acted like you wanted to move up, and you weren't going to let anything stand in your way." I paused for a second. "Including me," I added.

Liam nodded slowly. "Yeah, I guess it might have looked that way. I *was* feeling competitive," he admitted. "I felt like I had this opportunity, and I wanted to get everything out of it that I could. I've been interested in journalism ever since I was about three years old."

"Oh, come on," I said. "You didn't even know what the word *journalism* meant when you were three."

"Oh, I *did*," Liam said. "My dad was a total news junkie. We'd watch together every night, and he'd try to explain stuff to me. I even had a crush on our local weatherperson." He sighed dramatically. "She was really cute. Blond hair, blue eyes—actually, she looked a little like you!"

"Don't change the subject," I told him. "We were talking about news junkies. So what does your dad do? Is he in the business?"

Liam's face fell. "No. He was a carpenter. He died a few years ago. I really miss him."

I looked at him and put a hand on his arm. "I'm sorry," I said quietly.

Liam nodded. "Thanks," he said. "He was cool. We used to really talk—not like some kids and their parents. You know?"

"Yeah," I said. "I know. My parents are pretty cool that way, too."

As I unlocked the car doors, Liam gave an appreciative whistle.

"Speaking of cool," he said, "nice wheels." He turned to me, grinning. "Who chose the color?"

"Believe it or not, it was my dad," I told him. "But I think he got the idea from Ashley. She loves pink."

"And what's your favorite color?" Liam asked as he slid into the passenger seat.

"Actually, I don't have a favorite color anymore," I told him. "It used to be blue, but now I like them all." I laughed. "Ashley would say I lack focus."

"Oh, I don't know about that!" Liam said. "You've been pretty focused on the job."

"Not as much as you," I told him.

"Well, we need some focus right now if we're going to find those presents for your friends," Liam said. "Let's try Bruno's Used Books. It's over on Lakeland."

I turned the key in the ignition and backed out of the parking spot. As I turned to check behind me, I sneaked a peek at Liam. I couldn't believe he was being this nice and this helpful.

Liam McCaffrey was certainly turning out to be different from what I'd expected.

"Hello! Is this Mrs. Douglas Waterhouse?" I said into the phone.

Lauren stood next to me and gave me a thumbs-up sign. "Good luck!" she mouthed silently.

"Yes. This is she."

"This is Ashley Olsen," I said. "I think you spoke to Liam McCaffrey about me?"

"Oh, yes, of course. You're the one who's looking for Angel."

"That's right. I'm so sorry to bother you, Mrs. Waterhouse. But if you could possibly get a message to Angel—"

"Oh, honey, it's no bother. I'm bored to tears in this place. Talking to Angel will be the highlight of my week. What do you want me to tell her?"

"That the Valentine's Day dance at Bayside High has been changed to next Friday night, February fourteenth, and that she should call me whenever she can."

"Friday the fourteenth. And call you. Consider it done. I'll find Angel and call you back."

I gave Mrs. Waterhouse my cell-phone number. Lauren was cheering silently in the background.

"Mrs. Waterhouse, I just want to thank you again—"

"That's perfectly fine, Ashley. Any friend of Liam's is a friend of mine, as they say. He's a great boy. I've known his mother since we were in grade school together. I'll talk to you as soon as I contact our target."

I hung up the phone with a sigh of relief.

"Success?" Lauren asked.

"So far so good," I said. "Now I just have to wait for Angel to get the message. It looks like things might work out after all! I only wish . . ." My voice trailed off.

"I have a feeling things are going to work out for you and Aaron, too," Lauren said.

"I hope you're right," I said. "I'd feel better about it if he'd take my calls."

"Give him a little time," Lauren advised. "He's a guy. And if Aaron is typical, guys can be pretty slow. Like Ben!"

"I know, I know," I said. "Anyway, with a little luck, Angel will be free on Friday night, and everything will work out fine for the dance. I just hope Mrs. Waterhouse calls me back soon. This waiting is driving me crazy!"

chapter fourteen

It was quiet at the *Girlz* magazine offices. Nearly everyone had gone home. But I was there late, using my desk as the perfect place to wrap presents.

I finished tying a big red bow around Aaron's rubber ducky. It was a weird shape, and the wrapping job wasn't up to Ashley's standards, but it would have to do.

I took out a piece of Ashley's purple stationery I'd brought along. Imitating her handwriting and her way with words was pretty easy.

Dear Aaron, I started writing. *Quack, quack, quack. I've been a real turkey, ducking out on you when all I want is to be with you. Forgive me? Love, You-Know-Who.* At the last minute, I had decided to sign all the notes as *You-Know-Who*—actually forging my friends' signatures felt wrong.

I hoped the note sounded enough like Ashley—and that it would make Aaron smile. I folded the stationery and put it into a matching purple envelope. One down, five to go.

I chewed on the tip of my pen. Imitating Aaron and the other guys was going to be harder. I looked at some cards I'd bought that I thought a guy might send. Aaron's was romantic, Ben's was sweet, and Malcolm's was funny and a little sarcastic. The problem was going to be imitating each guy's handwriting and the way each of them sounded.

Faking notes from Lauren and Sophie was almost as bad. I knew them a lot better, but could I write notes that sounded as if they'd written them?

I pushed Aaron's present to the side of my desk and went on wrapping. I had gotten some blue-striped paper for Lauren's present to Ben. I cut it neatly into a rectangle and wrapped it around Ben's CD. I folded the corners of the paper and taped them down. Then I put a tiny dab of Lauren's favorite perfume onto the package. I had picked up a sample from Viv's office. *A brilliant idea, if I do say so myself,* I thought. Now the gift would even smell like Lauren.

I dabbed a bit of perfume behind my ears. *Mmm,* I thought. *This is actually a nice scent.*

"Getting ready for a date?" a male voice said from right behind me.

I whirled around. There, wearing a pair of jeans and a dark blue T-shirt, stood Liam.

"What are you doing here?" I said. "Or do you live here these days?"

"Yeah. My mom kicked me out of the house," he said with an innocent look. "How about you? You moving in, too?"

"Nope," I said. "I'm wrapping the secret Cupid presents. I got some of Lauren's perfume to put on hers. I thought it would make it more convincing."

"Ah," Liam said. "Very smart, Mary-Kate. And you smell good, too."

I sat forward in my chair and put my elbows on the desk. "The biggest problem is the notes," I told Liam. "I mean, I can imitate my sister pretty well, right down to the handwriting. But the others—especially the guys—well, that's different. For one thing, I can't really write like a guy. Plus I don't know what they'd say. And these have to look real."

Liam thought for a moment. "You know," he said, "you should go back and listen to their interview tapes again. That'll give you a sense of how each of them thinks and sounds. You might even find a phrase or two you can copy."

I had to admit that was a good idea. "I'll try it."

"And then," Liam went on, "if you want, I can write the guys' notes for you. I may not be able to imitate their handwriting exactly, but at least I write like a guy."

"Would you?" I said. "That would be so great."

"Just jot down what you want each one of them to say," Liam said, moving out of the office. "I'll be at my desk when you're ready."

After Liam left, I reached into my bag and pulled out the tapes of the interviews. My tape player was on the windowsill.

I popped a tape in at random. I pressed the button.

"Interview with Aaron Moore, side two," my voice said. "Okay, Aaron. Tell me more about what you think makes the perfect couple."

Aaron's voice filled the room. "I don't know about the perfect couple," he said. "But I can tell you a lot about the perfect girl—your sister. Ashley is . . ." Aaron's voice drifted off for a moment. "Ashley is the greatest. That sounds so lame. But it's true. It's not that she's beautiful or anything. She is, I mean. But it's how she makes me feel. Even when things stink—if I'm doing badly in school, or I just blew a goal in a big game or something—she always makes me feel like things are gonna be okay."

I turned off the tape. I couldn't believe how much my article had warped the truth. Aaron was crazy about Ashley. And it was the same thing with the other couples. I didn't have to listen to their tapes again to know how wrong I had been.

What I was doing just had to get them all back together. It had to!

❋

"Hello? Hello? Who is it? Is somebody there?"

I heard a *whooshing* sound on my cell phone. I rolled off my bed and walked to the window. Cell reception was sometimes better there.

"Hello?" I said again. "Who's there?"

Suddenly a voice came through the phone, loud and clear.

"Is this Ashley?" the voice said. "Ashley Olsen?"

"Yes," I answered. "Who's this?"

"Angelica Velasquez," the voice said. "Mrs. Waterhouse gave me a message to call you?"

"Angel!" I almost yelled into the phone. "Thanks so much for getting back to me!"

"Thank Mrs. Waterhouse," Angel said, laughing. "She was . . . well, let's just say she was very insistent about talking to me. She says the date of the dance has been changed?"

"Yes," I told her. "I'm so sorry. It's this Friday. Will you be able to make it?"

"Sure," Angel said. "I'll have to check with my band, but I'm sure it'll be all right with them. Actually, Friday is a little better for me. I'll be there around seven. Okay?"

"Totally okay," I told her. "And, Angel, thanks so much!"

"No problem, Ashley. See you then. Bye."

"Bye," I said.

I clicked END.

I raced to the head of the stairs. I just had to tell someone. And there was Mom, on her way up.

"Ashley? Is everything okay?" Mom was holding an envelope.

"Better than okay!" I shouted, racing down the stairs. I grabbed her around the waist and gave her a huge hug. "I just talked to Angel, and we're on for Friday!"

"Oh, I'm so glad." Mom hugged me back. "I know how worried you were. Dad will be pleased. And so will Mary-Kate."

"Mary-Kate!" I said. "I've got to call her right away." I turned to go upstairs again.

"Ashley, wait a second. This was just hand-delivered. It's for you." Mom held out the envelope she had been carrying.

"Who's it from?" I asked her.

"It's a little mysterious, actually," Mom replied. "There's no return address on the package."

She handed it to me, and I ripped the little tab across the top. Inside was a beautifully wrapped package and a small envelope.

I opened the envelope very carefully, my heart suddenly pounding. There was a Valentine's Day card inside. I opened it. Then I looked up at Mom.

"It's from Aaron!" I said excitedly.

Mom smiled. "That's good news, right?"

I stared at the card. Inside, my heart was doing little backflips of happiness. "Yeah," I said softly. "I think it's really good news."

Mom kissed me on the forehead. "I'm glad things are working out, sweetie. I'll be downstairs."

I rushed back up to my room and closed the door. Then I looked at the card again. It had the sweetest pictures of little angels and cupids all over it. Inside was printed, PLEASE BE MY VALEN-TINE. Aaron had written a note, too. *Dear Ashley*, it read. *Roses are red. Violets are blue. I'm not much of a poet, but I love you. Can you ever forgive me? Love, You-Know-Who.*

I fell back on my bed, the card clutched to my chest. *Oh, Aaron!* I closed my eyes. *Of course I can forgive you.* I reached for the phone to call him just as it rang.

"Ashley?" It was Aaron's voice on the other end of the line.

"Oh, Aaron!" I said breathlessly. "I just got your note. And the present! I haven't even opened it up yet, but I know it's going to be perfect, whatever it is. It doesn't matter, anyway. Of course I forgive you. I've missed you so much. I can't believe we let a little thing like an article in a silly magazine break us up."

"Whoa, Ashley," Aaron said, sounding a little confused. "Slow down! I feel the same way you do. And I was just calling to thank you for *your* present. But I didn't send you anything. I sure wish I had. But I didn't."

I stopped short. "You didn't?" I paused. "Did you say *my* present? For *you*?"

"Yeah," Aaron said. "The rubber ducky. Quack, quack, quack." He definitely sounded like he was smiling.

I sat up. "Wait a minute, Aaron. There's something fishy going on. I do love you. But I didn't send you a rubber ducky. I didn't send you anything. And if you didn't send me this"—I tore at the wrapping paper—"this framed photo of us, then who did?"

"I don't have a clue," Aaron said.

I thought a moment. "I might," I told him. "But I think we should call Lauren and Ben and Sophie and Malcolm before we do anything else. I wonder if they've all gotten presents, too."

"I'm beginning to get the picture," Aaron said. "If you call the girls, I'll get hold of Ben and Malcolm."

"Good. I'll talk to Lauren and Sophie, and then I'll call you right back."

"Great. There's just one more thing." Aaron hesitated. "Ashley, no matter who sent these presents, I do love you. I really do."

My heart did another backflip. "I love you, too, Aaron. I'll talk to you in a little while."

"Okay," Aaron said. "Call back soon. Bye, Ashley."

I hung up the phone and immediately dialed Lauren's number. Then I called Sophie. It didn't take long for all of us to figure things out. I was pretty sure now who was behind the sudden gift-giving.

chapter fifteen

I started up the path to my house, feeling better than I had in weeks. I knew my secret Cupid idea was going to pay off. Maybe Ashley and Aaron were already back together!

I walked through the kitchen. Mom and Dad were standing at the counter. Mom was peeling carrots while Dad chopped onions.

"Hi, Mom! Hi, Dad!" I said.

"Hi, Mary-Kate," Mom said.

"Hey, Mary-Kate." Dad sniffed. "Could you hand me a tissue, sweetie?"

I grabbed the tissue box and gave it to him. Then I walked into the living room.

There, sitting on Mom's blue-and-white-flowered sofa and staring straight at me, were Ashley, Aaron, Lauren, Ben, Sophie, and Malcolm.

"Uh, hi!" I gulped. "Um, what are all of you doing here?"

All six of them pulled out their presents and cards.

"You are so busted, Mary-Kate," Ashley said. But her blue eyes were sparkling.

"What were you thinking?" Sophie shook her head. "Did you really believe you could get away with it?"

Lauren nodded. "All it took were a few phone calls to figure the whole thing out."

"You know, Mary-Kate," Ben added, "forging documents is illegal in this state."

"Yeah," Malcolm drawled. "What do you have to say for yourself, young lady?"

I looked from one pair of eyes to another. They all stared back at me. Aaron even looked serious. But the corner of Lauren's mouth twitched, as if she was holding back a smile.

"Well," I said, half afraid of the answer, "did it work?"

Aaron laughed out loud. "Yes, it worked," he admitted.

Lauren grinned. "It certainly broke the ice. Once we started talking again—"

"We realized how much we'd overreacted," Aaron went on. "None of us gave anyone a chance to explain."

"Which is not to excuse your part in all this," Ashley added.

"Believe me, I know," I said. "And I'm so sorry about the article."

"Well, you made up for it with Mrs. Waterhouse," Ashley said.

I looked at my sister. "Angel! Did she call?"

"A few hours ago." Ashley got up and gave me a hug. "Thanks, Mary-Kate. If you hadn't gotten us Mrs. Waterhouse, we probably wouldn't be having a dance."

I looked around at my friends. They all looked happy, and I was glad for them.

But they couldn't be as happy as I was.

Everything had finally worked out for my three "perfect couples."

This year's Valentine's Day dance was back on track and on the way to being the best Valentine's Day event ever!

And there was something else.

I caught Ashley's eye. She gave me a wink, and I smiled back at her.

Ashley and I were back on track, too. And to me, that was more important than anything!

❁

Angel stepped back from the microphone as her band rocked on. She had silver streaks in her curly dark hair, and she was wearing a red and silver minidress with silver heels. Red was definitely her color.

I stood on the sidelines, moving to the beat. All around me couples danced, talked, and laughed. It was perfect.

The gym was decorated with red and pink crepe paper bows and streamers.

Pictures of Victorian cupids and angels were plastered everywhere. Angel-food cupcakes decorated with pink candy hearts, along with the usual chips, pretzels, punch, and soft drinks, sat on long tables along two sides of the gym.

"Great dress, Ashley!" Melanie whirled by me in one of her Paris creations—a black velvet strapless gown with a big green bow on the back. "And Angel is amazing!"

"Good job, Ashley!" added Jeff Green, her date for the night. "This music really rocks."

"Thanks!" I said happily.

Someone put his hands over my eyes. "Guess who?" a familiar voice asked.

"Aaron," I murmured, turning around.

"How'd you know it was me?" he asked, taking me into his arms as the music turned slow and dreamy.

"Just a wild guess," I said into his ear. "Quack."

Flash! The photographer from *Girlz* magazine snapped our picture.

123

"There's not a whole lot of privacy around here, is there?" Aaron grumbled.

"Oh, come on," I teased. "It's for a good cause, after all. Mary-Kate's editor is letting her do a follow-up piece about the real us. The least we can do is let them take a few pictures for their magazine."

Flash! Flash! Flash!

"A *few* pictures?" Aaron laughed.

We danced for a moment more. Then, as the song changed, Aaron pulled away. "You know, even though Mary-Kate exaggerated some of the things she wrote in her article, we do have to talk about it," he said.

"I know—but not tonight," I said, putting my head on his shoulder.

"Not tonight," Aaron agreed. After a few minutes, he took my hand and led me off the dance floor. "There's something I want to give you," he said. "Come with me."

We went out into the hall and stood by a window. A silvery full moon lit the night sky.

Aaron took a small box out of his jacket pocket.

"This is for you, Ashley," he said. "And this time, *I* bought it. Not Mary-Kate."

My fingers shook a little as I undid the wrapping and opened the box.

Inside was a beautiful silver charm bracelet. Hanging from it was a single heart-shaped charm.

Aaron looked down at me. His eyes were intense and very blue.

"Will you be my valentine, Ashley Olsen?" he asked.

My heart soared, and I had to blink back tears of happiness. "Of course I will!" I said, looking up at him.

Aaron bent down to give me a hug. I put my arms around his neck and drew him close.

Then Aaron picked up the bracelet. "I'll put it on you," he told me. "But I have to show you something first."

The heart-shaped charm was actually a locket. He opened it, and I saw that there was something engraved on the inside.

"Read it, Ashley," he said gently.

I read the tiny, perfect letters aloud. "'For Ashley. Love and kisses, Aaron.'"

I smiled. "Oh, Aaron, I love it," I told him. "Thank you so much."

Aaron took the bracelet and fastened it around my wrist. I looked down at it. It glittered against my tanned skin.

"It's beautiful," I whispered.

"Not as beautiful as you are," Aaron said.

I smiled up at him, and he smiled back. "Happy Valentine's Day, Ashley," he said.

❀

"Great dance, Mary-Kate!" Liam said over the music. He was standing by one of the refreshment tables, watching Angel sing. "She really is awesome! Thanks for asking me."

"Who asked whom?" I yelled back at him. "I seem to remember you asking *me*."

"That does sound sort of familiar." Liam grinned.

"Have you gotten a chance to interview Angel yet?" I asked him as the music died away.

"Yeah, we talked a little after the first set," he told me. "And I'm going to talk to her again before she leaves. I spoke to her dad, too. He was terrific. He showed me his team's trophies and told me all about how Angel's career got started. It's going to make a great story, Mary-Kate."

"I'm glad, Liam," I said. "You deserve it. If it weren't for you, this whole thing might never have happened."

"Oh, you and Ashley would have worked it out somehow," Liam said. "Listen, would you like to cowrite the Angel interview with me? After all, if it weren't for *you*, *I* wouldn't be here."

"I'd love to!" I said.

"Good," Liam said. "One more question."

"What's that?" I asked as Angel started to sing a romantic ballad.

"Would you dance with me, Mary-Kate?" Liam asked.

I looked at him. "Dance with you? Aren't you supposed to be working on your article?" I teased.

"Oh, come on," he said, laughing. "A guy can't work all the time!"

He held out his arms. I curtsied, grinning, and moved into them. Liam was a good dancer, and it felt comfortable being with him.

I relaxed. All was definitely right with the world. Ashley and Aaron, Lauren and Ben, Sophie and Malcolm—they all were back together. In fact, they were all dancing together right now. The Valentine's Day dance and Angel's performance were smash hits. I had one article already published in *Girlz*, with two more on the way—the follow-up to my "Perfect Couple" story and now the Angel story with Liam. I just knew C.K. would want to publish that, too. After all, I was on a roll!

Ashley danced by with Aaron. She was looking up into his eyes, and he was looking down at her as if she were the only girl in the room.

She glanced over and saw me. She flashed me a quick grin.

She and Aaron might not be a perfect couple. There was probably no such thing.

But it looked as if there would be plenty of love and kisses in their future.

And, someday soon, I knew there'd be love and kisses for me, too.

Find out what happens next in

Sweet 16

Book 14:

SPRING INTO STYLE

"Let's go check out the make-up, Ashley," Melanie said. She tugged me over to Glitter & Glam's make-up counter.

Glitter & Glam is one of our favorite boutiques in the mall. It has the most amazing stuff. Today, they were featuring the latest CrashBox line of make-up.

"Try that glittery bronze eye shadow," Melanie suggested. "It'll bring out the blue of your eyes."

Melanie always knows what's going to look good. She's the most fashionable of our friends. And no wonder—her father is in the fashion business. He's always bringing back the coolest clothes from Paris, Milan, and Tokyo for Melanie.

I picked up the tester and applied a bit to my left eyelid.

A dark-haired woman in a great-looking orange plaid suit hurried over to us. "Hello, girls," she said. "My name is Jennifer Lewis. I'm the owner of Glitter & Glam."

"Oh, we love your store, Ms. Lewis!" Melanie exclaimed.

Ms. Lewis smiled. "The mall is running a teen trend-spotting contest during spring break. Would you two like to be in it?"

"A trend-spotting contest? What's that?" I asked.

"Trend-spotters are people who keep their eyes open for anything and everything that might influence fashion," Ms. Lewis explained.

"Things like music, celebrities, movies, sports—even clothes you see other kids wearing. Whatever might turn into the next hot fashion trend."

"People get paid for that kind of thing?" Melanie asked.

"Yes. In fact, there are lots of teens all over the country who have part-time jobs spotting trends," Ms. Lewis said. "You girls wouldn't be paid for this, but the winner of the contest will get a shopping spree in her favorite store."

A shopping spree? I couldn't think of a better prize! "That's payment enough for me!" I told her. "Where do I sign up?"

Ms. Lewis handed us some applications and a meeting schedule. "Just fill in this form. . . ."

"This whole thing sounds amazing!" I said, taking the papers.

Ms. Lewis's eyes lit up. "Oh, I'm so glad!" she said. "I knew you'd both be terrific trend-spotters the minute I saw you. I mean, that vest, for instance," she said, pointing to Melanie. "Vests like that are the hottest thing in Europe right now. But we don't expect them to hit here until next spring. It's very cutting edge."

"Oh, um. Thanks," Melanie said.

I was surprised. Melanie *loves* talking about clothes. But she didn't sound very excited.

Suddenly Melanie handed the papers back to Ms. Lewis. "I'm really sorry, but I just realized. I have a job this spring break. I won't be able to make it." She turned to me. "Ashley? I need to pick something up at the drugstore. I'll see you there." She turned and hurried out of the store.

I stared after her. A job? I happened to know that she *didn't* have a job this spring break. *What was up with Melanie?*

mary-kateandashley

mary-kateandashley

Sweet 16

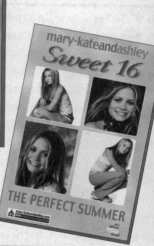

(1) *Never Been Kissed*   (0 00 714879 8)
(2) *Wishes and Dreams*   (0 00 714880 1)
(3) *The Perfect Summer*   (0 00 714881 X)

 HarperCollins*Entertainment*

 PARACHUTE PRESS

 DUALSTAR PUBLICATIONS

 mary-kateandashley.com
AOL Keyword: mary-kateandashley

mary-kateandashley
TWO of a kind ™

HarperCollins*Entertainment*

PARACHUTE PRESS

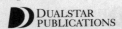
DUALSTAR PUBLICATIONS

mary-kateandashley.com
AOL Keyword: mary-kateandashley

mary-kateandashley

TWO of a kind ™

 HarperCollins*Entertainment*

 PARACHUTE PRESS

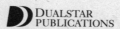 DUALSTAR PUBLICATIONS

 mary-kateandashley.com
AOL Keyword: mary-kateandashley

Mary-Kate and Ashley collections now available!

nick.co.uk

NICKELODEON'S CRAZY ABOUT MARY-KATE AND ASHLEY

With Mary-Kate and Ashley shows, competitions, movies and much much more... check it all out on Nick.

AOL. **mary-kateandashley.com**
AOL Keyword: mary-kateandashley

NICKELODEON